Bedlam
In
Bellagio

Balloonificent

Bookstore

For my amazing husband James, for encouraging my writing, and indulging me in all the nonsense we have participated in since the first day we met in 1986.

Chapter 1

Lake Como sparkled in the sunlight. The scenery was stunning: majestic mountains reflected in the deep blue water, while the colourful villages and towns nestled below.

It was Saturday, in May, and boats floated about on the lake, their skippers no doubt enjoying the afternoon spring sunshine. Perhaps they were on holiday from the sweaty city, content to have escaped to such scenic surroundings.

As I wandered along the lakeside in Bellagio, looking for the ideal place to enjoy the view, I spotted the lakeside café. The café appeared just at the right moment as it was time for my afternoon coffee. It was precisely the type of café I wanted.

The waiter, pristinely dressed in black trousers and an immaculate white shirt, showed me to a table beside the lake's edge. This table was perfect. From this position, no one could pass by me to interrupt the superb scene. I heard the sound of the lake, gently waving in the slight breeze, and smelled the freshness of spring.

This was picture postcard scenery; I used to send postcards on my travels, but nowadays you load the holiday pictures straight onto social media! Everyone shares their holiday instantly with the world. I always find this a tragedy, but I'm guilty of complying!

I decided to take the picture but not share it—well, not at once, perhaps by dinner time! I hovered my camera and snapped various zoom-in and zoom-out versions. I liked to think I took a good picture. The scene was so perfect that I wanted to touch it, turn it over, and write "Wish You Were Here" on the back.

The thought made me smile ruefully. Who did I wish were here?

I didn't plan this Bellagio weekend as a solo break. Frankly, I wasn't averse to my own company or scared to travel alone. Independent was my middle name. However, I'll tell you what happened and why I ended up in Bellagio alone. It's quite a tale; I know I must go through all the details as this story unfolds. I promise I'll not hold anything back. I understand that certain people won't like what I'll divulge, and they will never do what I've done.

I know this may depend on their life experience, which is fine. Everyone has a view of life depending on what's happened to them. Self-analysis can be exhausting, and it's right for others to voice their opinion freely. We're not all the same; it takes all kinds to make a world! So, I can take all views on board.

So here goes, *deep breath*, rightly or wrongly, I was having an affair (well, yes, I know it's wrong!). Well, when I say I was having an affair, I couldn't quite decide if 'affair' constituted the description from my perspective, as I was single. He was married. (Various dictionaries' definitions would say otherwise – "*a sexual relationship between two people, usually when one or both of them is married to someone else*"). So, he was having an affair with me, and I was complicit in this enjoyable time. Okay, I concur, I was having an affair!

I know it sounds as if I was confused, but my investment in this affair was minimal. I'm not trying to excuse my behaviour, or am I?

Having male company now and then was convenient for me. However, if I were in a committed relationship, that would be inconvenient when I like to be as free as possible. So, seeing someone without having all the ties and neediness was attractive to me.

In my early twenties, I married Keith. He was my opposite, and believe me, opposites don't attract. We fought like cats and dogs. On rare occasions, we still see each other because we have two sons, Jack and Dan. Our sons are now adults, so we no longer need to be in each other's company very often.

If Keith said 'black,' I said 'white.' If Keith said 'shit,' I said 'shite.' When we first met, it wasn't clear that our relationship would progress to disaster. We're both intelligent, however, in different ways. He's artistic and creative, and I need to give him the accolade of having more common sense than I. I'm logical and more emotionally intelligent, but I lack willpower!

Once we bought a home together, the cracks started to appear. The wonderful arrival of our two boys gave us a common hope. However, by the time the boys were four and two years old, we could see that it wouldn't work. We both took comfort in making life the best for the boys. I'm incredibly grateful for this, but it doesn't make us get along. Keith married again, and they are a perfect match! I prefer good sex I can walk away from and no commitment in my busy life.

In this affair situation, I could walk in and out for the fun part. However, it was annoying when a secret getaway you planned went pear-shaped, then you had to grin and bear it.

Tim, the guy I was having an affair with, had a daughter. His daughter had an accident on the way to school on Friday morning. This was the day we were supposed to fly to Milan and then travel onward to Bellagio on Lake Como. It was no one's fault, in simple terms, a child comes first. My two sons still come first if they've a problem, so I completely understood Tim's responsibility to his daughter that morning.

You might think he was hedging and took cold feet about the thought of a clandestine weekend away. I appreciate why you might think this, but I knew, in this situation, he wanted to go with me. In fact, he seemed overly keen. Every time we met up, he talked incessantly about it.

I know! I hear you! I know, what you're thinking – if his wife found out then the shit would hit the fan. It was unfair to her. This was true, and I suppose, perversely, there was excitement in the danger of someone catching us.

However, I put my sheer disregard for his wife to the back of my mind, as I was willing to go out with her husband. I realise when I speak of this, I sound cold-hearted.

Have you ever been in a position where you believe you're a nice person? I convinced myself I didn't know Tim's wife. I tried to make this a good reason for allowing myself to act like this.

Was I a complete bitch? Was my inner demon overtaking my ego? Who knows? Why do we do things for momentary pleasure? We take the adrenaline rush for a few moments of joy, then debate whether it was all worth it!

Everyone has their guilty pleasure; the temptation they succumb to. Although I suppose if it's chocolate, it isn't the same risk except to your waistline, your arteries, and the chance of diabetes. There I was rationalising this affair versus death by chocolate. I suppose pleasure, which doesn't affect people's lives, is one thing, while my actions could cause harm, and I refused to think about it.

I reckon people don't want to admit their guilty pleasure or face it head-on! Or they've brilliant willpower, which, for me, was low on my list of skills! My accumulated skills didn't include resisting handsome men.

I woke up that Friday morning and jumped out of bed. There was a spring in my step. I usually go for a run; however, I decided I was in holiday mode and just concentrated on getting ready. I was excited. I had my legs waxed, Brazilian sorted, and my nails manicured the previous day. I was prepared for a dirty weekend! Tim and I were due to meet at the airport at 10 am.

Then a text arrived from Tim.

"Need to speak to u asap."

I intuitively knew disappointment was on the cards. The taxi was picking me up in less than an hour to go to the airport. I called his number, and he answered.

"Iona, I'm so sorry I've bad news, Lara's school has phoned, and I'm on the way to the hospital, she has broken her arm and...."

"No need to say anymore, Tim, is she okay?"

"Well, in pain, but seems to be. I'm so disappointed."

"Tim, don't even go there; you must put your daughter first!"

"Oh, you're the best, Iona. You're always nice, which is why I was looking forward to this weekend. I can't believe it isn't going to happen!"

"Oh, I'm not that nice, remember, I'm the other woman!" I replied half-jokingly.

"What will you do, now?" asked Tim.

I didn't hesitate too long, as I was looking forward to going to Italy. I was ready for the spring sunshine kissing my face. "Well, I might as well go anyway!"

"What! Are you going to go without me?" Tim asked, he sounded injured but also annoyed.

"Well, yes, there is no chance of getting the money back, and I'm all set for the Italian sun. I've the time off work too."

"But this was our trip together, I thought we'd rearrange for next month!" Tim replied.

"Well, I'll go over and suss it out for us," I said.

"I can't believe you're going to go," he moaned.

"Tim don't start this nonsense; I can do as I please, and so can you. I'm going, and we can go again or somewhere else," I said firmly.

"Yes, but you better watch yourself with all those hot-blooded males, they might try and steal you away!" Tim said, trying to sound funny, but I could hear he was mad.

"Hey Tim, I'm in my forties, and there will be young supermodels with exotic figures. I don't think I'm in danger of an Italian man snapping up," I told him, laughing.

"You underestimate how attractive you are. Remember and come back to me!"

The comment was annoying. He wasn't mine to return to, just as I wasn't his. And the fact was that if a gorgeous, hot-blooded Italian did by a tiny chance sweep me off my feet, I wasn't sure I'd resist. You know what I mean if you're single. Even the thought or anticipation of meeting someone new fills me with excitement. I love a good flirt with a handsome man, who doesn't?

But he was already upset about his daughter and about not getting to go on a wild weekend with me, so I let it pass. This wasn't the time to argue.

"Oh, I'll be back Tuesday night, and if all is well, I'll see you Wednesday afternoon as usual?"

"I'm upset you're still going!"

"Tim, take care, and I'll see you next week. You can text me over the weekend and make sure I'm in bed at 9 pm every night!"

"You know how much you mean to me."

"Bye, Tim."

I hung up. I wasn't getting into that conversation—the "*how much you mean to me*" nonsense. It was a path to doom. If this affair became too deep and emotional, the fun would disappear, and we would be in danger. If we started to talk about a future together or wanted to look at a more meaningful relationship, I'd call time on it.

I was annoyed because I didn't want a meaningful relationship with Tim. I could tell he was suggesting I shouldn't go and stay at home. But do what? File my nails!

I couldn't deny it was good to feel like a silly teenager again, going on a trip, laughing, and getting up to all sorts of things. However, I never wanted this situation to progress beyond acting like a teenager. Sometimes, his comments worried me. Recently, he'd made similar, lovestruck comments. I ignored them when possible, but they irritated me.

I fixed my lipstick in my hall mirror and smiled at my matching luggage. I resigned myself to the fact I was on my own, off to the Italian Lakes, and funnily enough, I still felt extremely excited about this trip.

The taxi arrived, and the driver helped me out with my suitcases. He gave me the usual look as he lifted the heavy case and wondered what the hell I'd packed. I packed for every eventuality. As far as I was concerned, it was better to have and not need than need and not have!

I locked the front door, sat in the taxi, and waved to my house, telling it I would be home on Tuesday! The holiday started when I locked the door and was on my way. I loved every aspect of travelling. When I arrived at the airport, I was just as excited as I would've been if Tim had been with me.

Chapter 2

Now sitting at Lake Como, I felt a heady happiness. A woman liberated, who, at this time in her life, had the freedom to make her own choices and be bold. There was lots to explore and 'me' time to enjoy! However, I could imagine Tim sitting opposite me with his handsome face in the sunlight.

There was no denying he was a good-looking guy and fit. So, he and I would've had great sex if he were here with me. We probably wouldn't have made it down to dinner the first night ending up in bed in a frenzied shag like the way it happened on a Wednesday. I reckoned we wouldn't have slept the first night. We would've come up for air in the morning needing food. However, I wondered if being in each other's company for longer than usual might've become boring!

We didn't know much about each other beyond revealing the best parts of ourselves in this clandestine relationship. In an affair, you meet your lover looking your best. You make the extra effort for the few stolen moments you get to share. However, you don't reveal all your standard parts. Your habits, the things you find annoying, your personality traits, and the things that drive you are missing from the puzzle. So, you see the other person as the perfect version of themselves, but, as we all know, no one is perfect.

I thought about when Tim and I met. We were at a training seminar, sent by our respective employers. The course involved talking about teamwork, coaching, and engaging with internal and external stakeholders. I'm sure many of you've been on a course like this! Tim had sat next to me.

There was a touchy-feely session where you had to massage the person next to you on their shoulders. I know people who hate this level of tactile approach, and it's well out of their comfort zone, but I was okay with it. I usually found it fun. It was optional whether you joined in. I had better make that clear.

Tim and I laughed as the course coordinator explained what we had to do. We made eye contact, and there was no awkwardness between us. When he touched my shoulders, there was a spark. Then it was my turn to massage his shoulders, and he told me later that the feeling was mutual.

It was a residential course. We went to dinner with all the other delegates, drank wine, and chatted. The chit-chat at these dinners is always general about where everyone works and opinions about the course. One by one, the others bid us goodnight.

There are all types of people on these courses who have their preferences. There are the ones who go straight to bed after dinner, others allow themselves one drink then leave to call their other half, and people like me who fear missing out and stay till the last ember has extinguished in the fire – metaphorically speaking. Tim and I found ourselves to be the last ones standing.

You can guess what happened next: we ended up in my hotel room.

What a night we had! We just clicked. It was lustful and passionate, a spontaneous night of great sex. We never slept a wink. At no point did either of us consider the other person's circumstances. We'd not asked each other about it during the day or evening. Perhaps we didn't want to know. It was one of those nights that unfolded, and, in that moment, you throw caution to the wind as if tomorrow might not happen.

After experiencing the heady delights of that night, I found out Tim was married, but by then, I had enjoyed the experience and wanted more. Had I known this fact before the Earth moved, would it have been any different? Would my conscience have gotten the better of me? I can't answer. I don't know.

What I did know was it was lust. I could separate lust from love. My feelings were to shag him when I saw him. He was pleasing to my eyes. However, I didn't want to be with him every minute of every day. Initially, the thought of being with Tim existed. I spent the first three days daydreaming about doing things together after we met. Romantic dinners and long walks would all end up in bed; however, that passed quickly. My busy work life soon replaced the dreamy state, and looking forward to seeing him a couple of hours a week was enough for me. In the back of my head, I probably already removed the thought of anything more due to his marriage. I wasn't interested in getting involved beyond the fun part.

I knew I'd not fallen for him in any other way apart from my Wednesday afternoon fix. We were both out on the field for work, so this was easy to arrange over lunchtime. I know it sounds cold when I explain it like that, but if I spent too much time in Tim's company, he'd likely annoy me. He said things and had opinions I found irritating, as well as habits that would annoy me if they came into my daily radar. I could ignore these because I didn't spend much time in his company.

The best thing about the Wednesday afternoon rendezvous was the thrill of secretly meeting. I'd never spent a weekend with him. In hindsight, agreeing to this trip may have been a mistake. So perhaps it was better that we weren't in each other's company 24/7 on a weekend break. When I agreed to come, the attraction was partly coming to Italy. I decided without considering whether it was the best idea overall.

Anyway, I was alone in Italy, and it felt fantastic.

Chapter 3

I had an article to write for work. I'd decided to bring my laptop at the last minute. Once I knew Tim wasn't coming, I thought I might as well throw it in the hand luggage.

I brought it with me to the café. Sitting with my laptop, typing away and drinking an espresso, I felt like a mysterious novelist escaping for inspiration to the Italian Lakes, needing time alone with her art. I'd had a habit of imagining and daydreaming. What's more relaxing than a good daydream and letting your imagination run wild?

At school, my thoughts would wander out the window to my daydreams and fantasy lands. Then the teacher would ask a question, and I wouldn't recall what she had been talking about! This happened to me throughout my life. I would drift off when someone was talking. I know this doesn't appear polite, but my thoughts drift without knowing I'm doing it.

In all honesty, I was drafting an article about why consumers invest money and manage to keep it invested, while others don't have the appetite for long-term investments. Someone might put ten grand in a stocks and shares ISA, which decreases slightly due to market turbulence. They withdraw the funds the next minute as they can't cope with the decrease or wait long enough for it to recover. Others can go in for the long term and not bat an eyelid. I call them a 'Nerves of Steel' investor. They don't shake when the stock market does.

This article was for a company magazine. It was hardly romantic content, but I loved that people wandering past might wonder what I was writing about.

I was qualified to write about this. I promise. I had the necessary certification in this field. I had also invested with remarkable success over the last fifteen years. Since my divorce, I've committed to creating a bright future for my boys and me. I can't deny that Keith, my annoying ex-husband, provided for the boys, which helped. However, I wanted to create an independent lifestyle and stand on my own two feet. I was a financial adviser, so I knew about wealth creation. I smartly invested and managed to build up a substantial portfolio. I still lived well, but invested a monthly amount of money and treated it like a monthly outgoing, plus any bonuses, and extra funds coming my way.

I was also fortunate to receive an inheritance. I instantly invested these funds before the thought of blowing it on an around-the-world cruise took over me.

I did look up the cruise for the boys and me, dreaming of the far-off lands. I imagined us in every port from here to Australia, travelling with new outfits and carrying matching luggage. However, I convinced myself, at the time, they were too young to appreciate such grandeur. The investment of the inheritance funds would provide lifelong help for them at various stages of their life when they needed it most. So, although I said earlier I had no common sense, I suppose I did with this logical stuff. It was more when it came to men and craving excitement, I threw caution to the wind.

The temptation to spend on other foolish things arose, but I kept going. 'Nerves of Steel' – I had to live by this motto as I coached my clients to do the same. It is all about balance and having a good life while ensuring your future wealth.

Now, I could reap the rewards from my endeavours while continuing on the trajectory of retiring early. Various finance magazines and companies invited me to author articles about wealth creation for them. This was due to the reputation I developed with my client base. I invested all the proceeds from this additional work, too. To date, my portfolio is worth £750,000. This didn't include my pension fund, so I was delighted with myself.

I celebrated where I was on my financial journey. I allowed myself to shop for new clothes for this weekend. I wore a gorgeous beige, Ralph Lauren dress with tan wedged sandals. The hairdresser curled my blonde hair the day before, and I finished my look off with my Gucci sunglasses. I felt like a million dollars! It was good to treat yourself once in a while. Let your hair down and feel the best you can. I did dress well for work, but you'd find me in leggings and a t-shirt at home the rest of the time.

I finished my espresso. I was hungry. I had breakfast at 8 am It was large, but now it was well after 1 pm, and the hunger pangs weren't noticeable. I was about to ask for a menu from the pristine waiter when my mobile started ringing. The caller ID showed the caller as "Adult Child 1."

"Bonus Daius," I answered.

"Hi mum, I can't find the hair straighteners."

It was my 22-year-old son, Jack. All of a sudden, I felt as if the lake moved away. I was teleported home to my living room. The place where I had to know the answers to all the questions. From where the clean pants were to when the universe began! Even as Jack approached twenty-two and Dan was just behind at twenty, it was like having a couple of toddlers. It was a military operation to leave home for five days. I had to write everything down. When to feed the cat, what to eat, and where all their clothes were. I drew the line at the GHD straighteners, though. They were mine, and it was a delusion on Jack's part thinking I would leave them behind, for him to use, for a whole weekend.

"Jack, where do you think they are?"

"Uh, in the drawer?"

"No, funnily enough, they are here with me in Italy."

"Are you in Italy? I thought it was France! Oh, Mum, did you take them with you?"

"Well, Jack, did you think I would spend five days in Italy without doing my hair?"

Jack laughed heartily. "I'll just need to resort to wax till you get back!"

"Well, you could always buy yourself a pair!"

"What, spend £100 on straighteners, you must be joking! Have a fun time, Mum."

"Thanks, Jack, enjoy the weekend."

I smiled as I hung up. They would be planning a big house party in my absence. The house would be mayhem when I returned. Still, I was glad that was how they were. It seemed right that my kids were party animals. I liked a good party myself. I like all their friends, a great crowd of young people, so I wasn't worried about them gathering at our house.

They didn't know about Tim, though. They would be unhappy about that. My boys would absolutely question my actions with Tim. This made me cringe just thinking about it.

I honestly felt more guilty about my boys not being aware of what I was up to than I did about Tim's family. I managed to remain detached from thinking of Tim's home life.

A text message arrived as I tried to attract the waiter's attention so he could bring me a menu. I knew it was from Tim because I had the sound for Tim's text messages and phone calls set to a low, dull tone, as if people might discover the affair if it were a jolly tone ringing.

"R U missing me?"

Mmm, I didn't know if I was missing him. All this time available for reflection on this trip was making me think. Had I missed him at any point since I left home? When I got on the plane, I had a gin and tonic and a snack box, you know the one with the olives, cheese, and biscuits?

I had a window seat, so I could see the Alps as we came over the top and down into Milan. It was stunning. I arrived early afternoon, and the weather was divine. The pre-booked transfer taxi was waiting at the airport for me to take me to Bellagio. I enjoyed the journey and the beautiful scenery. It was thirty-six miles to Bellagio from the airport. The driver tried to converse with me in broken English, and I responded to him with the limited Italian I knew. We laughed. He was older, but he was a handsome man. He had dark features and a twinkle in his eye.

He was charming and fun, and I was in a great mood when I entered the hotel reception.

The hotel was exquisite, the Grand Hotel Villa Serbelloni. Tim and I picked it, one Wednesday afternoon, as it looked so beautiful in the photographs. It sat on the edge of Lake Como. It has a history. Count Frizzoni built it in the 1800s as a luxurious holiday villa. Then, when it became a hotel, JFK and Winston Churchill visited it.

It was expensive, but we booked it for four nights of sheer decadence. When I walked through the front door, I knew it was special. They treated me like a queen on arrival and escorted me to my room. The porter brought my matching luggage using a bellman baggage cart. I went into the hotel room, and there was a view to die for! I stared out the window for ages, soaking up the scene. The porter offloaded my luggage, and I tipped him. I usually tip far too much on the first day when trying to work out the currency conversion in my head. He seemed happy with my offering and left smiling.

I freshened up and changed before going downstairs. I chose a seat on the hotel terrace, overlooking the gorgeous lake and ordered a bottle of red wine. I sat there soaking up the early evening sun, which kissed my face.

I finished my evening with a fantastic meal in the hotel restaurant. The food was delicious and highly satisfying. Dining alone was great as you could savour every morsel without chatting. I had a thing about this – talking while eating. I liked to eat without saying a word!

I felt fabulous travelling alone, with time to think, enjoy my own company, and do exactly as I pleased. I was at a time in life when I was confident and fearless.

So, was I missing Tim? The honest answer was no. Tim's presence here would've made it a different weekend, but I had no complaints.

I knew I wouldn't be that blatant about it. Being tactful rather than truthful was sometimes the best policy. In this instance, I went for tact. He was the one who was missing out. I replied, "Not the same without you x."

That way, I never said anything one way or the other.

"R u lonely?"

God, why could he not just accept the first reply? *Lonely*? No, I didn't feel lonely; I was sitting in impressive surroundings without a care in the world.

"It is gorgeous scenery, Tim, I'll take photos, and we'll come here next month!"

That should do it.

Right back came another text,

"You know u are so special to me."

Hell, I didn't want to be his special thing. The situation was convenient for me, but I couldn't say this to him. He was handsome and pushed all the right buttons on the physical attraction front. However, I didn't want conversations about unrequited love with him.

"Looking forward to seeing you on Wednesday, I'll bring a present from Italy for you to enjoy! x."

"Take care, sweetheart, I wish I were there xx."

There was no need to send any further replies. I sighed as if I had just finished a hard day's work. Should I end this clandestine affair with Tim? Was he getting in too deep with all his sweet comments, or did he feel he had to say these things to be nice? I couldn't decide. I wasn't good at letting go of the passion – I did enjoy the Wednesday rendezvous. I put all these thoughts to the back of my mind for now. At last, I summoned the waiter to bring me a menu. My hunger was real!

He was a waiter from the old school of waiterism. I think I've made this word up. He was profoundly serious and attentive, and I was scared to mispronounce what I wanted to order. Or to request a stupid combination of food because I may receive a look of supreme disapproval. In my humble opinion, Italy was the birthplace of the waiter, so I needed to be on my best behaviour. I didn't want to use the wrong fork or pick up a panini with my hands. I was breaking out in a cold sweat as I told him in Italian that I wanted a mushroom pizza. "Posso avere una pizza ai funghi, per favore?"

He understood me so, I felt very clever! I knew in Italy that I shouldn't request silly toppings on my pizza. You never ask for peppers, onions, mushrooms, and chicken on one pizza. That is like asking to dance with the devil in Italy.

Then I asked for a glass of red wine. It seemed right to order a side salad with a dressing.

He looked at me sternly after every item, nodding his head slowly. Oh, please don't give me a row, I thought. When I finished, he snapped his fingers. Waiters surrounded me. A fresh, crisp tablecloth, a napkin on my knee and a wine glass appeared. The waiter poured a splash of the wine for me to try. *Oh, god, pour me a big glass.* I tried the wine; it was delicious. I did the swirly thing with it and gargled it around my gums like you do with mouthwash. Although I tried not to make the gargle noise! I smiled and nodded my head. The waiter awarded me my proper glass size based on my approval. It was a conveyor belt of perfect service.

My laptop had now taken up residence on a chair beside me. I then relaxed, sipping my wine while the pizza baked in a proper pizza oven in the café's kitchen.

"Phew," I thought, "I had passed the ordering test."

It is funny how travelling alone doesn't bother me, but dealing with a professional waiter is traumatic. When I was younger, I stayed at posh hotels while travelling for work. It was the era of nouvelle cuisine. I ordered chicken and mashed potatoes, and the food arrived, covered by a vast, silver-serving dome. The two waiters approached the table carrying it. It looked like they were about to serve me an enormous feast. I sat there in anticipation as it reached me.

The waiters poised in front of me, one holding the plate, the other ready to lift the giant dome, about the size of St Paul's Cathedral. They looked at me as if I should applaud the situation. Underneath would be a beautifully fashioned food sculpture. However, it was about the size of a postage stamp! I was still starving after I ate it!

Anyway, back to Lake Como, where the spring afternoon sun was hot. I was glad of the parasol above my head, placed there by another attentive waiter. I could smell the pizza as the waiter made his way over to my table. The waiter supported the pizza above his head with one hand. He landed it like a well-piloted jumbo jet right in front of me.

A giant, fabulous, stone-baked Pizza, perfect to enjoy in these exquisite surroundings, made in the fatherland of pizza. It couldn't get any better than this.

I intended to savour every last piece of pizza washed down with wine. I don't think I could ever recall such a perfect Saturday afternoon. I was in a joyful zone.

I would lock this moment in my heart as an ideal moment to reminisce if I ever needed to cheer myself up.

I set to work on my delicious lunch. As I dissected each portion, the mozzarella stretched into long strings. I gazed at the stretched cheese like a possessed child. Why was mozzarella mesmerising? Although I loved cheddar, Cheddar never performed, when melted, the way mozzarella did! It bubbled while mozzarella could extend for miles. I tended to play with it, lifting my fork up and down and watching the stringiness before eating it. It was like food Play-Doh! It tasted heavenly. I was in Pizza Paradise.

This always happened to me when I was eating. I loved my food. I told you earlier that I'd rather not talk while eating. When I started to eat, I could ignore everything around me. There could be a fight, and I'd sit eating my dinner oblivious to what was happening.

Once, after a long train journey, I arrived to meet a business contact. I was hungry, so he suggested a café to have lunch before our meeting. I remember going into the café, but once the pasta I ordered arrived, I metaphorically climbed into the bowl and forgot I was dining with someone else. As the last piece of penne crossed my lips, I looked at the guy's stunned stare. I realised I'd ignored him as I devoured my lunch.

So, it was no surprise to me. I was eating this divine pizza and completely tuned in, not paying the slightest attention to what else was happening.

Who was coming in and out of the café?

Who was walking down the street?

What were the little boats doing out on the lake?

Eventually, the last portion of pizza sat on my plate, and I was traumatised because this would mean THE END. The end of my pizza paradise, but I didn't want it to finish yet. The flavour, the taste, and the satisfaction from each bite had me locked in. Slowly, I forked the final bit and raised it to my mouth, placing it in and chewing the last lovely morsel. Slowly, I let it digest, and then my pizza was gone! Finished!

I needed to breathe and take a sip of my wine. My hunger was gone, and I was truly satiated. My focus returned to the café's reality from that gorgeous plate. Dabbing a little grease off the side of my mouth with my napkin, I reached for my wine glass. I was back in the room. The hypnotic pizza trance was over.

I looked around, glancing at the table beside me, and nearly fell off my chair.

Chapter 4

A Hollywood actor was sitting at the table opposite me. He stared right at me with a massive grin on his face. This wasn't just any Hollywood actor. He was my favourite.

Was I mistaken?

If I weren't suffering from pizza overdose hallucinations, then the gorgeous hunk of humanity looking directly into my space was Mike Maloney.

How could this be? Mike Maloney was within grabbing distance of me. I could reach out if I wanted and touch him, squeeze his being, and rough him up. Well, not exactly rough him up, but you know what I mean! Oh my, just an absolute dream of a man to look at.

Do you know the feeling when your mouth opens and shuts? Words come out, and you wonder where they came from. Well, this was such a moment. He was still staring at me, but I had no idea why I cheekily said, "Would you like a photo?"

"Only if you can pose with another mouthful of pizza," came the reply in an American accent, from his smiling mouth, with the whitest teeth and lips you could kiss forever.

Oh, he was cheeky. I loved it. It was too much. This ideal moment had just escalated beyond anything I could ever imagine.

"Well, if you want to order another pizza, I'll see what I can do," I replied. Again, where were these words coming from? I felt elated; I was talking to Mike Maloney. No one would believe me when I told them this happened to me.

"Or if you've had enough pizza, you could always invite me to join you, and I'll share this bottle of wine with you to help you wash it down." He indicated the bottle of wine on his table; I could see it was from this region, Valtellina Superiore Inferno.

Mike Maloney wanted to join me at my table and bring me wine! Was this a dream? It must've been my pizza brain; I'd gorged too much. I was in a dough-brain state. I'd wake up in the hospital after they'd pumped my stomach. Although it seemed real enough, he looked real sitting right in front of me.

Come right over handsome fucker!

"You may join me if you're bringing wine!" I answered, then let out one of those giggles from your soul's depths. I hoped it didn't sound like a giant burp. My heart was doing a Formula One race. Why was I able to pretend to be calm and collected? My 'Nerves of Steel' were useful on this occasion.

He stood up and motioned to the waiter, who attended, lifted the wine, and then fetched a fresh glass for me.

Mike was stunning. He was wearing a simple black Armani T-shirt and jeans. He had an aura about him. I know Mike's fame may cloud my judgement, but I could sense good energy from him.

I could see what a well-toned body lay underneath his clothes. He came towards my table, grinning like a Cheshire cat. His handsome face sported a shadow beard, setting off a gorgeous smile. I couldn't take my eyes off him; he could've melted the hardest heart!

I was sitting in the café with Mike Maloney on a Saturday afternoon in Bellagio. It was surreal. I was counselling myself to remain calm and not talk utter shite to him.

"Why were you so hungry?" he asked, laughing once he settled into the chair opposite me.

I thought he might say the cliché, '*Why is a lady like you dining alone?*' I was so glad he didn't say that!

"I've only been released from prison and have been eating bread for 10 years!" I replied. The on-tap responses must have been forming in my vivid imagination!

"Mm, what were you in prison for?"

"Bad Behaviour!"

"Oh, and did you get out early?"

"No, I didn't improve my behaviour for early release, I served the whole sentence!"

He laughed heartily.

"I'm Mike." He stretched out his hand to shake mine. *Oh, I fucking know who you're, you gorgeous beast.*

Taking his marvellous hand, I could feel the tingling as our skin touched.

"Iona."

Chapter 5

We held hands for a few seconds longer than necessary. Sparks were flying through me as if someone had wired me up. The twinkle in his eyes was tangible as he locked on mine. The waiter interrupted this spell by filling my glass with wine.

"Well, Iona, we need dessert. Since you've been in prison for 10 years, I presume you've not had any treats."

"You're correct, Mike, I spent nights in my cell dreaming of a tiramisu mountain where I lie on the top and eat my way to the bottom!" *Was that too far?*

Mike roared with laughter, obviously it wasn't too far at all! It wasn't a fake laugh; it was infectious, and I joined in.

We ordered a tiramisu to share.

In the space of ten minutes, I'd made acquaintance with the famous Hollywood actor Mike Maloney, touched his hand, shared his wine, and awaited the arrival of a dessert to share with him. *Please don't wake me up from this dream!*

"So, it's Saturday afternoon, and you're in a café with your laptop, having just left prison. Would I be correct in deducing that you're a writer, getting inspiration from this majestic view?"

I smiled. He thought about what I imagined people would think when they saw me typing on my laptop. Marvellous!

"Well, I'm a financial adviser. It would be much more fun to pretend I'm writing a murder mystery!"

"Fine, I'll accept that you're a murder mystery writer under the guise of a financial adviser. Are you going to write me into the book then?"

I laughed aloud. *I want to do more for you than write you into a book, mate*! I moved on swiftly.

"And you, it's evident that you're a Hollywood actor having a break filming and enjoying watching strange women eating pizza in your spare time?"

"I come down here specifically for that purpose, and boy, did I get a show today –I've never seen such an attack on a pizza."

We laughed again. It felt relaxed considering the short amount of time we'd spent together. I enjoyed the witty chat; it wasn't romantic but, hell, it was making me feel like a horny angel.

"And to add, it sounds like you're from Scotland. How lucky can a guy get?"

"Oh, you like Scottish ladies, do you?" I questioned him with a glint in my eye. "I'm certainly from Scotland on a weekend trip here."

"Luckily, I decided to come to town today, or I might've missed you. Are you here with family or friends? Do they know you've been released from prison?"

I laughed.

"No, I'm here myself. I'm having an affair. The guy I was supposed to be coming here with had a last-minute family crisis and couldn't come. When I say I'm having an affair, I'm single with two adult sons, so he is the one who is married." I blurted out.

Too much information. *Why the hell did I tell him all that?*

"Fuck, tell it the way it is! I like a woman who lays her cards on the table," he laughed.

Thank goodness he laughed!

"Were you upset he couldn't come?"

"No, I was just thinking I'm having a wonderful time, and it feels good to have my time to myself."

"Do you feel bad for his family?"

"I should, but I don't, which sounds cold. It's only physical for me, but I think he's getting feelings for me, and I don't want that."

"Ah ha, an independent lady who only needs physical interaction. Should I be scared"?

"Very," I said, laughing wickedly and taking a large swig of wine. I hoped I'd not laughed too loudly. Do you know the wine-fuelled loud laugh when you believe that you're functioning at a normal volume?

He laughed, then asked, "So, what about your sons?"

"Oh, they don't know about the affair! They wouldn't be happy about that. They think I'm ancient! Their dad and I split years ago. We weren't in love, just in competition with each other, to see who could win each argument we had!"

"In the past, I've been in a relationship like that! However, let's discuss 'Ancient'. You look terrific, I can tell you're a natural beauty."

"Wow, Mike, you certainly know how to make a girl feel good."

I loved the compliment. I was floating.

He was handsome, but he was also a nice guy. Despite his fame, he didn't seem to have a massive ego, which pleasantly surprised me.

"So, are you here for a long break, Mike?"

"I'm here for two weeks. I flew in on Thursday, so I've another 12 days to spend. I'm hosting a big party Friday night for all my friends. I've got this crazy party coordinator involved, and he's driving me mad. His suggestions for entertainment are off the planet. At one point, he suggested bringing in an ice rink with skating ducks! I told him I had business to deal with in town. He will be great at organising the event and is doing a marvellous job, but he's crazy! You should come to the party!"

I spluttered on the wine I had just sipped.

"What me!" I tried to laugh, but it came out like a shriek.

"Why don't you behave at parties, Iona?" he teased.

"No, I don't! I usually somersault on the floor and over the back of the furniture. And I must sing!"

"Then you should come," he laughed heartily.

"Just one small problem, I'll be back home by then; I leave here on Tuesday morning."

"Well, I've until Tuesday to convince you. You could stay on until the weekend or fly back out on Friday.

I giggled. "Oh, that would be naughty of me. Everyone would think I was off my head. I would need to tell them I was jaunting back to Italy for Mike Maloney's party three days after I got home from Italy. Just for the hell of it, I might!"

"Great, we can have fun now since I won't need to spend time persuading you. That is, if you want company?"

Did I want company?

Spending time with Mike Maloney in Bellagio? He was a Hollywood Actor who wished to hijack my solo weekend and have fun with me. And he needed to ask if I wanted company? This was a dream.

"Wait until I consult my social diary for the next few days. Yep, it seems clear, I'm available to have fun! Of course, my idea of fun might not be the same for you!"

"Well, tonight we could go up to a mountain restaurant where the view is to die for and enjoy gourmet food and wine. It is a winding road up, so you need to be a good traveller! I already know you like food!" he laughed.

"Well, so far so good, I'm a seasoned traveller of long and winding roads, and I do love food," I replied, spellbound. The thought of a dinner date night with Mike stimulated my senses. "But how do we get there?"

"My driver will take us."

Of course, he had a driver to take us! How the other half live!

I was now tipsy from the wine.

"What shall I wear?" I wondered aloud, then felt stupid.

"Wear whatever you please, ma'am. You look lovely the way you are, but I know a lady always likes to change."

A lady, he called me a lady. I giggled more and realised I needed to get a grip on myself.

We sat silently at the lake for a moment, but it wasn't awkward.

Then Mike asked, "Do you like water skiing, Iona?"

"I'm willing to try it!" I replied, "My one skiing experience was on the slopes at Glen Shee in the North of Scotland, but I haven't ventured onto the water with skis. Are you going to teach me?" I asked cheekily.

"I might," he winked at me, "I take it you can swim?"

"Yes, I'm a great swimmer. They throw children in the water when they are born in Glasgow to ensure we're strong enough to survive the winters!"

Mike threw his head back and laughed. I wanted to climb onto his knee and kiss his handsome face.

"Okay, I had better get back to the villa and see what Emilio, the party planner, is up to. Where is your hotel, or are you staying here for now?"

"No, I'll head back to the hotel. I'm staying at the Grand Hotel Villa Serbelloni; it isn't that far."

"Oh, you can't hide good taste!" he winked at me. "Okay, I'll walk with you, then I can get my boat back to the villa. The skipper moored it down at the jetty."

He made a quick phone call to the skipper of his boat and spoke in Italian. I was weak at the knees. I tried to pay for my Pizza. It felt like I had eaten in a different lifetime, but Mike had already added it to his café account. He said it was the best pizza he had ever experienced without eating a slice!

The time was 3 pm. We waved goodbye to the waiters, who didn't seem nearly as serious anymore! We walked onto the pavement. Mike put a protective arm on my shoulder to guide me through the Saturday crowd. I felt I might melt at the touch of his hand on my shoulder. As I walked along, I wanted to rest my head on his shoulder, but resisted being too familiar. Especially in my wine, pizza-fuelled state of heaven.

It became clear Mike was a familiar face around the town, and the locals were cool with it, but the tourists were all agog. Between the café and the hotel, tourists stopped us six times asking for an autograph or a photo. Mike was patient and kind when talking to people. It was funny because I could have been anyone on his arm; they were so intent on speaking to him that I could stand back and watch, admiring his charm. He didn't have a massive ego. It was marvellous to see this is who he was.

We eventually arrived at the hotel entrance, and I started panicking about what to do next. Should I ask him for coffee or invite him to my room – too presumptuous?

Luckily for me, he got a call back from the skipper to tell him the boat was ready.

Mike looked at me and touched a wave of my hair blowing in the wind.

"Iona, I'll meet you at the hotel reception at 7.15 pm. I'm so pleased I met you and experienced your pizza heaven," he laughed.

With that, he gently held my shoulders and kissed both my cheeks. He then gave me the most fabulous smile and walked away towards the jetty, turning once to wave.

Chapter 6

I can't remember the journey back to my room. I stopped at the reception and picked up my key. Envious women were staring or perhaps glaring at me, but I didn't notice. I went into the room and threw myself on the bed. I let out little screams of delight, then giggled hysterically for about 10 minutes.

What had just happened over the last two hours was out of order, totally crazy. I had a dinner date tonight with Mike Maloney!

Bloody hell!

Then I thought too much about it, and I started to doubt. He wouldn't turn up. He does this every Saturday afternoon. He preys on women dining alone, watching them eat pizza, filling them with wine, and pretending he will take them to dinner.

But then – what would be in it for him – doing that – it isn't as if he took advantage and then promised dinner. Maybe he likes the thought of a woman getting ready and then letting her down.

Then I laughed at myself for doubting him. Of course, he would take me out for dinner. He even walked me back to the hotel. I wasn't usually like this, but it wasn't the typical situation you typically find yourself in when you go to a café for a pizza!

Thank goodness I went shopping for clothes before I left. Okay, it wasn't Prada or Versace, but I knew there were decent dresses in my suitcase that looked good on me.

A text came in from Tim.

"What R U doing, sweetheart? X"

Oh, I'm going out to dinner with Michel Maloney, he has just kissed both my cheeks!

Imagine I had sent this as a reply. It would seem like the rantings of a mad woman. Should I have felt guilty about this? No, I didn't think so, as Tim was having an affair with me. I wasn't his girlfriend, so I believed this wasn't cheating. However, I was happy to keep this on a need-to-know basis rather than face a barrage of text messages all night.

"Back at the hotel. Thinking of going for a swim," I replied.

That was true. I decided I might go for a dip and rejuvenate after all the pizza and wine. I wanted to feel fresh for the date with Mr Maloney.

"What are you doing tonight – it should be us going out for a romantic meal."

Shit!

"Going out for a meal. XX"

This was true, not a word of a lie.

Hopefully, the kisses would reassure Tim, and he would leave me alone so I could enjoy myself.

"Where are you going to go?"

What sort of question was that? He had never been here before, so if I told him the restaurant name, it wasn't as if he would know it.

"Somewhere local xxx"

Still true enough, I considered going up the mountain as local to Bellagio!

"Good, I don't want you venturing too far when you're alone. You can let me know when you're back in your room. X"

I was annoyed! I wasn't letting Tim tell me what I should do. I could hardly be cheating on a man who was already cheating on his wife anyway!

I hadn't seen this side of Tim before; it felt controlling. I didn't like a control freak! Or had he been like this all along, and I missed the signs? My ex-husband annoyed the life out of me, but he was never a control freak!

"I'll be fine."

"U, okay? That last text seemed a bit short."

It was only three words, of course, it was bloody short.

"I'm fabulous. I'll bring you a present on Wednesday. My battery is about to go. I'll text later. X"

"Okay, sweetheart, wish I were there, X."

I didn't wish that. Not anymore, not when I had time to think about it more. Taking a step back from daily life provided me with clarity. I was beginning to think that being in Tim's presence for too long might prove suffocating. It is weird to step back from a situation and consider all the aspects. You see flaws you hadn't realised existed.

Tim and I met on a Wednesday afternoon. We were in amongst the hustle and bustle of daily life. It was a chance for downtime in amongst the daily dramas. I hadn't thought about how he might act outside that bubble we met in!

I accept that meeting Mike in the afternoon was an unexpected event that may have disrupted my thoughts. However, since I'd arrived in Bellagio and before meeting Mike, I pondered our affair.

I sent a few texts back and forth to my boys. I was desperate to tell them who I'd met, but I kept it all a big secret. I was unsure they would share their mother's enthusiasm for a forty-something actor. At home, I'd only suggest that a guy on the television was gorgeous for the boys to start shouting:

"OMG, did you need to say that?"

and

"Enough information, mum."

I was supposed to be in the wallpaper, available to comfort and provide food as required. There was no need for me to have desires and dreams. I didn't blame them; I acted similarly at their age.

I decided to have a long soak in the large bath rather than swim. I didn't want to smell of chlorine. My hair would've protested too and refused to calm itself, no matter what products I applied. My hair doesn't like to go on holiday!

The hotel provided candles and luxurious toiletries in the bathroom. I set the tap running and created the most delicious bubbly bath. Afterwards, the enormous fluffy hotel towels were ready to wrap myself in.

I rolled my hair up in the big rollers to give it bounce, letting the steam from the bath curl it slightly.

I lay in the tub and let the heat radiate deep into my bones, soothing away the journey, the travelling, and the tension of my muscles. I wasn't tense in a bad way, but because of all the excitement, I was tensing up without realising it.

I fell into one of the daydreams I mentioned before. It was the best daydream ever, and I drifted into a dreamy sleep, floating on a bubble cloud of bliss.

I woke with a start. Where was I? Did I dream I met Mike Maloney? What time was it? *Oh shit.* I grabbed the luxury towel, jumping out of the bath. I wrapped it around me, but stubbed my toe on the bathroom door as I entered the bedroom. I yelped out in pain and started crying like a baby because it hurt. I was desperate to get to my watch and check the time. I thought I had missed my date.

I hobbled across the room, whining like a child. When I checked my watch, it was 5.30 pm. I started to laugh hysterically. I had plenty of time to get ready. I glanced in the mirror; my rollers were still intact, apart from one hanging on my shoulder, and my mascara had run from my tears. I poured myself a large glass of sparkling water from the glass bottle provided in the room. Then, I sat on the edge of the bed rubbing my throbbing toe.

I smiled, thinking of the night ahead and spending it with Mike Maloney. My head was starting to hurt slightly, due to the wine I had drunk earlier. I took two paracetamol – no headache was going to waste this night out!

Chapter 7

The Roman gods must have looked down upon me and granted my wish that my hair would style perfectly. After all, Bellagio was a Roman settlement. I'm sure Jupiter and Juno were looking down, not to mention the Roman god of love, Cupid. I was sure the Roman gods made my hair look like a Vestal Virgin's. They probably wore their hair up, but I imagined it would look like mine down. Yes, I know Virgin is a bit of a stretch considering I had two kids and was having an affair, but I played along with my daydreaming.

Cupid was sprinkling love dust on me – I was sure of that. So, with my lovely Roman curls, I needed an equally devastating dress. It was a pity it wasn't a toga party I was going to! However, I had the perfect dress to complement my theme. It was a white dress, and I did call it my toga dress.

The top was the style a Roman goddess wore. *Well, they wore dresses like this in the Hollywood movies anyway!* It gathered at the shoulder and enhanced the bosom. Then there was a waistband around the middle, and the skirt tumbled down beautifully from it. It had an uneven hemline like Tinkerbell's skirt. I loved this dress the minute I saw it in the shop window. I was going to accessorise my look with gold jewellery and sandals.

I put on my makeup painstakingly, but it wasn't that painful. I loved putting on makeup.

I gazed at myself in the mirror. Self-appreciation was the key to your worth, I always thought. I looked straight into my eyes and smiled to myself. I wore the dress and jewellery and slipped on my golden high heels. Then I looked at myself again. Vanity somehow didn't seem sinful to me, but then what did? Oh, what the hell – I thought I looked stunning even though I said so myself.

It was 6.45 pm, and I thought I would venture downstairs and have a drink at the bar. I had a habit of always being ready early while impatiently waiting for everyone else.

There was never a suitable time to go downstairs in these scenarios. You wanted enough time to get down there and avoid any delays. On the other hand, being too early sometimes attracts unwanted admirers. This was such an occasion.

I entered the hotel bar.

"Bella Bella!"

Oh, dear, this one was a shouter. I had walked in and ordered a vodka and lemonade. The bartender did a fussy job of the ice, splashing in the vodka, lemons, lemonade, an umbrella, and a short straw. It did look lovely and refreshing. As I turned round, my "Bella

Bella" man was beside me. He was plumper than most, and his head reached level with my boobs. He did try to take his eyes off them.

"Why is a gorgeous lady drinking on her own tonight?" he asked with an Italian accent.

"I'm going out," I smiled, "My car is coming in 20 minutes."

"Oh, I've 15 minutes to convince you to stay with me. I'm Antonio!"

Oh hell.

I smiled again and tried to be polite. He was going to be annoying while I waited for Mike.

"Oh, Antonio, nice to meet you. Sorry, but as I told you, I'm going out. So, please don't waste your time on me."

Right enough, looking around the bar, I could see no other "free" women available, so whether I looked gorgeous or like Attila the Hun, I was the pick of a sparse crop!

"Ah, you're from Scotland. I've been to Scotland!"

"Which part?" I smiled back.

"Glasgow!"

"Oh, my, what a coincidence, I'm from Glasgow!" I said, giggling a little bit. I didn't want to have a fit of the giggles and offend him. When someone said they'd been to Glasgow, they expected you to know the person they'd visited.

"My brother has a restaurant there!"

"Does he? That's amazing. What's it called?"

"La Romana"

I knew it. It was nice. I had dined there before.

"I've dined at La Romana, Antonio; it's very nice."

"Oh, then you must tell my brother you spoke to Antonio next time you visit. His name is Lucio!"

"Next time I visit La Romano, I'll tell him."

I glanced out from the bar over the hotel foyer, and my heart skipped a beat. I saw a large car pull up. Onlookers were excited by its arrival. Antonio looked around.

"Ah," he said, "Mr Maloney has come to the town tonight, that is his car. You know Mike Maloney, the famous Hollywood actor?"

"Yes, Antonio, I know him. It is him I'm meeting. He is here to collect me."

Antonio looked at me strangely. He appeared shocked by this news, but he seemed to recover quickly.

"Ah, now I know why you don't want to spend the evening with me – I'm not from Hollywood," he pouted.

"But I've enjoyed speaking to you." I bent over and gave him a little peck on the cheek.

"You've not even told me your name?"

"Iona," I smiled as I walked away.

"Adios, Iona," he said like a wilting flower.

Chapter 8

Now I was floating out toward the most handsome apparition. Mike was at the reception desk, looking right at me. His smile was electrifying. He wore a white shirt and black trousers, style personified.

"Wow, Iona, you looked good this afternoon, but you look amazing." He then kissed me, and the touch of his lips on my cheeks blew me away.

"You look fabulous yourself," I giggled, and he laughed too.

"I thought maybe you'd stood me up for your friend in the bar," he said, amused.

"I was debating who to choose," I said. I loved being playful with Mike; it felt so natural.

"So, what swayed it for you?" He asked back, a twinkle in his eye.

"You've got a driver!" I laughed, and he joined in, putting his hand around my waist while guiding me out the hotel door. Flashing Lights blinded me.

What the hell?

It was the paparazzi. They now knew that Mike was in town, but I was shell-shocked. I forgot for a moment I was with such hot property.

"Just smile and get into the car," he said, reassuringly guiding me.

I smiled and entered the back seat as elegantly as possible while a camera flashed up my behind. Thank goodness I was happy with my look and wore lovely white knickers! It was exciting, and I loved the buzz.

Mike jumped in laughing, and we sped away.

"They have their picture, so I've told them they've enough photographs and information for this evening.

"Do they listen to you?" I asked.

"If you play them right, chat with them, and give them a little piece of what they want. This is the best way to work with them. It comes as part of being famous, and of course, they help you when you need publicity for a new movie."

I loved Mike's even-headed approach to this.

"Anyway, let's have some champagne and celebrate this glorious night in Italy."

Glorious, exactly how I felt. Sheer bliss!

The champagne bucket and flutes were all prepared. I just realised I was in a Bentley. In all the commotion, I hadn't paid attention to the vehicle. Mike and I were alone in the back of a luxurious leather-clad car. The driver was miles away in the front seat. Mike handed me a flute of champagne, and we clinked flutes.

"To a wonderful Saturday in Bellagio!"

"Cheers!" I said, smiling like a Cheshire cat.

We sat and sipped champagne in blissful silence. Dusk was approaching, and a full moon was making an appearance. I loved a full moon; it was a sign of completion and letting go.

"I never get fed up looking at the moon," Mike said. I loved that he noticed it too.

"Should I worry that your palms will get hairy?" I played.

"It's when I start chasing you through the woods, you need to worry!" he snarled, doing a werewolf impression.

I laughed, and so did Mike.

"I remember you were a werewolf in a movie?" I remarked.

"Oh, what? I can't believe you know this, my first movie," Mike laughed heartily.

"I watched it with my friends, and we were terrified. However, we all wanted to meet the werewolf!" I giggled, winking at Mike. "Wait till I tell them about my date with a werewolf!"

Mike poured more champagne for me and looked into my eyes.

"Yes, wait till you tell them about your whole evening spent with a werewolf!" he said teasingly. Then pulled me close and kissed my forehead. I wanted to pass on dinner at this point. However, I controlled my urges for now.

We had been winding up the hill, and the car was going slowly.

"I know I told you in the hotel, Iona, but you look stunning, like a Roman goddess in that outfit.

I let out a little squeal – he got the goddess thing – how fabulous.

Composing myself, I replied, "Oh, this is just a little dress I had!"

"If all your little dresses are like that, I want to see more!"

My phone rang in my handbag. I had contemplated not bringing it out with me. However, my overactive imagination got the better of me. What if someone needed to contact me urgently? What if the boys had an emergency? What if I lost myself in the Italian mountains and needed an air rescue? What if Mike doesn't give me a lift home, and I must call for a taxi? All these thoughts were in my mind when I decided to bring my phone. However, if Tim tried to contact me, I didn't want to speak to him. And I knew this was Tim calling. It was the ringtone I added to his number.

"Answer it if you want," Mike smiled at me warmly.

"Oh no, I don't know why I brought my phone! Whoever it is can leave me a message. I'm going to put it on silent."

I stuck my hand in my bag and fumbled for the sound button without looking at the missed call notification.

"Sorted," I said, "no more interruptions."

Mike filled up my glass again. The way he looked at me made me tremble. He gazed into my eyes, and it was spellbinding. He took my hand, entwining his fingers with mine. There was chemistry between us. I'd never felt like this. His energy was merging with mine.

"So, what story would this hand tell me?" he asked, lifting my hand and kissing it.

"This hand has been a few places and touched many things, some marvellous, some not so great!" I giggled.

"Well, you need to share one of the marvellous things with me, that's fair?" Mike teased.

"Oh," I giggled, "it's too early in the date to tell you."

"At what stage in the date would you divulge this information then?" he teased.

"Probably around the dessert menu," I smiled at him.

The conversation was easy, relaxed, and funny. It felt like the best daydream I've ever had.

We arrived at the restaurant, which looked like a scene from a romantic movie. The type of movie where the girl ends up with the hero on top of a mountain, eating pasta, and all is well. I don't know if such a movie exists, but in my head, it does.

The driver opened the door for us. Mike got out first, then extended his hand to help me. He was such a gentleman. I managed to exit elegantly even in my heels.

The restaurant was a stone building snuggled away on the hilltop, protected by trees on three sides but with a view of the Lake. It was inviting, and the smell of cooking from inside was divine. I could go in here with this gorgeous man and live happily ever after.

Through the windows, I saw the candle lights dancing on the tables, sitting elegantly on the crisp white table covers, their flames reflecting against the sparkling glasses. This was the type of place where romantic meals happened! Mike led me to the door with his arm on my waist. I floated through the door.

The waiter stood just inside the door. He greeted us warmly and asked Mike how he was. It was obvious Mike came here regularly.

I was in planet heaven. I never wanted the moment to end. I was treasuring every little part in my head for a rainy day. I could joyfully relive this day and evening forever.

The staff treated us like royalty. However, it was discrete. They showed us to our table and placed a bottle of champagne beside us before I could blink.

People at other tables made a passing glance. They had evidently been here before, and seeing a handsome Hollywood actor was normal. Only one couple openly gawked, their mouths hitting the floor.

The waiter handed me the menu. I could feel my phone vibrating in my bag again! I wish I hadn't brought the bloody thing with me. I thought that throwing it over the mountainside might be an idea. Tim would want to know where I was – poor me, dining alone. I took a breath- there was no pang of guilt – out of sight, out of mind.

I looked across the table, and Mike was looking at me intently.

"You've beautiful eyes," he said, "they are alive and shining like stars."

For once, I didn't want to say anything witty back. I wanted Mike to hold me in his gaze forever. I smiled, keeping eye contact. He reached across the table and held my hand.

"This day has been full of delightful surprises," he smiled.

Chapter 9

As I sat with Mike eating dinner, I had left the entire world behind. Except for when the waiters took our orders and served our meals, Mike and I were engaged in a brilliant conversation. I even managed to talk during the meal—not with my mouth full, of course, only between bites!

I love an enjoyable conversation, and this was a great one. It was a two-way conversation. Two people talked about life, and no one commanded the centre stage. Mike had a lot of interesting things to say. We were genuinely listening to each other. The chat flowed, the laughter came easily, the silent moments weren't awkward, the serious parts, the subtle questioning, the honest answers. I realised I hadn't had a decent conversation like this in forever.

Mike had a couple of earlier serious relationships. He had three kids in total whom he saw regularly. Someone had broken his heart once. *Me?* No one had broken my heart. I only realised this when Mike asked me the question. The beauty of this enjoyable conversation allowed me to reveal things.

Here was someone I had just met who was able to help me honestly reveal myself for the first time. I felt alive, refreshed, and invigorated by this discovery of myself.

As I talked to Mike about my relationship with Tim, I realised I was using it to remain stuck where I didn't have to put in too much effort—this place where I could enjoy sex once a week and an occasional weekend away.

It was a place where I didn't need to grow as a person in the relationship stakes. I could remain in the status quo, not having to make any effort to develop a mutual, satisfying relationship with anyone else.

This had been going on for three years. I had decided to place myself in this position as it made life easy. It let me have fun without it being challenging or time-consuming. I existed in a relationship vacuum, and there was no room for improvement. I realised this was due to my marriage to Keith. We mentally exhausted each other trying to win the argument. Embedded in my subconscious was the programming to avoid being in that scenario again.

As this dawned on me, I felt guilty about Tim's wife and family. I would stop this at once. I no longer wanted to be part of a situation that, long ago, I had convinced myself was okay. It wasn't okay! I needed to explore a new adult life that didn't involve encroaching on other people's lives or territory.

It was quite the conversation. Mike had listened as I poured out my soul to him. He had been the catalyst for an outpouring of emotion stuck inside of me, gluing me to a situation and allowing me to stick fast to it. He had been through a similar awakening a few years earlier, playing around in other people's lives, then one day he woke up and smelled the coffee. He discovered he didn't want his happiness defined by taking from other people. However, at no point did he judge me; we just talked and talked and talked, and it came pouring out. It was cathartic.

On the Italian mountainside, on a spring evening in May, on the most unexpected day I had ever lived, I felt as if I was reborn.

Chapter 10

We came out of the restaurant feeling like different people from the ones who walked in. There was an invisible bond forming between us. Was our meeting not as random as it seemed? Did the Roman gods play a hand in this fate? I did like this thought, Cupid sitting on a cloud. He saw me sitting at the café earlier today, and saw Mike coming over. He thinks," Oh, they would look good together," then points a finger from the sky and aligns us.

Yes, I've an overactive imagination.

Outside, nighttime had arrived. The Italian Spring night in the mountains had a slight chill. I shivered. We were the last to leave the restaurant, and neither of us noticed everyone else had left. Our conversation had kept us engrossed.

Our car was coming up the hill. You could see the lights. Mike turned me to face him. He stroked my arms with his warm hands, taking away the goosebumps. Then he put his hand under my hair to the nape of my neck. He pulled me in, gazing into my eyes. Then his lips touched mine. They were warm and inviting. I let out a small gasp. Then I reacted to his lips. Mine joining his, the warmth and strength of his kiss sending tremors through me.

Then his tongue was in my mouth, gently probing, and my tongue met his and probed back. Our bodies pressed against each other. He moaned as did I. He could carry me into the night and lose me forever, and I wouldn't protest. It was euphoric. His hands were on my back, gently kneading, massaging my soul. I pressed my hands into his strong upper back, feeling his strength. He let out a loud groan when I did this.

Suddenly, we heard an awkward cough. The driver had arrived.

Shit, I was enjoying myself!

I could hardly bring myself to pull away, and neither could he. We slowed down, but we were giving each other small, intimate kisses on the lips. Looking at each other, we both had twinkles in our eyes, which could have lit up the night sky.

We managed to separate while holding hands. I giggled like a naughty schoolchild. Mike cleared his throat. He nodded to the driver, who expertly opened the door, and we were in the back of the car. We acted like a pair of love-struck teenagers once more. The sheer joy of this moment was palpable. You could have reached out and felt the heat—the exchange of two new lovers in those first embraces.

I was feeling presumptuous at this point; we had only met and kissed, but I wanted to be his lover right there and then. I know there is an opinion that the first night isn't right. You should wait. I understand being coy! But life was too short for this level of sensibility on such an occasion. Caution to the wind wouldn't be the action taken if the offer of action were on the table.

I usually wasn't romantic, but this man was knocking me for six. I wanted to bottle it up and save this feeling. I was sure it wasn't just because of his fame.

Mike was a gentleman whose hands remained on my back above my waistline. He wasn't assuming anything.

We came up for air after a passionate kissing session. It reminded me of those long snogging sessions you had in high school at the school disco. Up in the corner with a boy you fancied, then a teacher would come over and separate you. The teenage hormones would be in full swing. Then you would walk home with the guy, sharing a bag of chips, and share another snogging session at your garden gate.

The car wound its way down the mountain.

"What would you like to do next, Iona?" asked Mike.

I giggled at this question.

Eh I was hoping we would go straight to the hotel and shag until the cows come home!

"Well, what are our options?" I replied, trying not to be too silly.

"Well, I wondered if you would enjoy a short sail in the lake in the moonlight," he smiled back.

This had to be a dream. Sailing on an Italian lake in the moonlight, with Mr Drop Dead Gorgeous, who also had an endearing personality.

"I can participate as long as I don't need to row!" I replied.

Mike let out a belly laugh.

"Ok, I'll take both oars then."

"It's a deal!"

Chapter 11

I didn't need to row. The car pulled up by the jetty, and I could see beautiful sailboats waiting to take lovers out on the lake. Mike guided me to a gorgeous sailboat. This wasn't a rowing boat in the local park's boating pond. I was sailing into the moonlight on Lake Como with a Hollywood actor.

I threw my head back and laughed like an idiot. I had no idea where it came from. Mike looked at me for a second, then continued to chat to the guy onboard, who I guessed was the skipper. They were grinning and nodding and doing that thing guys do. It is a guy thing; you know what I'm talking about.

I needed to pee. The whole evening, I couldn't bear to drag myself away from Mike to visit the toilet. He had gone once, but I just sat enjoying the atmosphere.

I was desperate for the toilet. I wish I had gone to the restaurant now! Why do you need the toilet at the most inconvenient time?

"Mike, where is there a toilet on board?" I asked, trying not to sound as desperate as I was to go.

Mike grinned at me. He put out his hand and hauled me onto the gangplank. I giggled again. What was with my giggling? I was seriously giggly around this guy. He told me to sit on the boat's edge. He then removed my killer heels.

"There is no way I'm letting you fall down those steep steps to the lower deck wearing these," he said,

I felt as horny as hell. He looked at me as he removed my shoes, his hands touching my feet. I was trembling. I've never considered someone touching my feet as sexy, but this was a new erogenous zone now. Usually, when anyone went anywhere near my feet, I was hysterical in case they tickled them!

Mike completed the shoe removal and offered me a hand up.

"The first door on your left at the bottom, you can't miss it," he told me.

Gingerly, I went down the narrow steps. The steps on boats are always so steep. I found myself outside the bathroom. It was small but well-kitted out. Thank goodness there was a mirror. My vanity was checking in to ensure I still looked good. I stood in front of it. My lipstick had vanished with us kissing, but I didn't care. I felt fabulous. I'm sure there was a glow around me. My puckered lips were ready for round two.

I was warm to the core. The closet with the toilet was beyond the sink. As with doors on boats, it was small, so I had to squeeze through. Once inside, I struggled to pull up my dress. I sat down and let out a big, contented sigh.

Then my overactive imagination started to play with me. What if this weren't Mike Maloney, but a clone? Was this someone posing as Mike to abduct me? Why did he happen to meet me at the cafe? Little old me, Iona from Scotland. A woman sitting there all alone. The taxi driver from the airport could have been in on it. He drove me from the airport and knew I was alone. Oh no, here I was below deck on a strange boat, trapped with a kidnapper. Then I remembered I had my phone. I scrambled to get it out of my bag. Frantically, thinking of how I could escape this abduction. I started to sweat. How did I get myself kidnapped? How stupid was I?

Then there was a knock at the door.

"Are you okay in there, Iona? Come back up top to see the lakeside in the moonlight as we sail off. I've a nice glass of champagne waiting for you!"

Mike's voice, I calmed down, and he wanted me to go back up to the top to look at the view. A kidnapper would've had duct tape over my mouth by now and stuck me in a stowaway box—my bloody imagination. Of course, he was the real Mike Maloney and all the trimmings that came with him. I pulled myself together and told myself to stop imagining things.

"I'm just coming," I shouted back.

My phone was now in my hand. I glanced at it and nearly fainted. One hundred missed calls! I frantically looked down the list in case there were any from my boys, but they were all from Tim. Oh, my goodness, he was finding it hard dealing with me being away. I seriously couldn't believe he had called me so many times. I knew I had to end this affair.

His attitude was unacceptable. It was supposed to be fun between us, and now it felt like he was a stalker.

I fixed my hair and reapplied my lipstick. I wanted to launch my phone overboard, and if it hadn't been for my boys, I would've. I decided to go upstairs to enjoy every minute of this fairytale evening and forget about the calls.

Now that I had returned to normal sanity and knew Mike wasn't a kidnapper, I made my way back up the steps.

There he was, standing in all the glory of the moonlight, Mike Maloney, handsomeness personified. He was smiling broadly and offering up a glass of champagne. I took it from him, smiling back.

He slipped his arm around my waist and gave me a romantic kiss, then took my hand to guide me to the front of the boat. It was slowly edging its way out of the marina.

We sat barefoot on the deck looking out as the boat edged out of the marina.

Mike turned to look at me.

"This night feels surreal," he said. I came out this afternoon for what I thought was a glass of wine in the sunshine. Now, here I am, sitting beside you, beautiful!"

He was so captivating.

"I can't believe it myself," I said. "I left home yesterday on an adventure on my own. Within 24 hours, I feel I've fallen into a romantic movie. But more than that, I never had such an enjoyable conversation with anyone as I've had in the restaurant with you this evening."

Mike laughed, "I was about to say the same. I've been to dinner dates where there was a lot of staring and silence, and then not much else."

We both laughed, and he put his arm around my shoulders, and I rested my head on his shoulder. Then we had a silence. However, this was the right kind of silence: content, satisfied, in the moment, with no need for words and mindful of the here and now.

Bellagio twinkled beautifully under the stars; the windows of the villas dotted around the lakeside were alight. We sat sipping champagne, enjoying the scene. As the boat got further out in the water, it was so quiet, as if only Mike and I were in the world. The boat's skipper might as well have been on another planet.

Suddenly, there was a flash, like a camera flash. It startled both of us. Then a voice—well, more of a gasp.

"Ah."

"What the fuck!" Mike shouted out.

As we recovered from the flash, a familiar figure stood before us.

"What the fuck," I said, "you are the man from the hotel bar earlier, Antonio!"

"Let me explain, please," said Antonio.

It was him. I could see his round frame in the moonlight. I thought he must be a paparazzi or something, but he was holding an iPhone, not a professional digital camera.

"You better make it fucking quick," Mike shouted, "and it better be fucking good!"

I could hear Mike's concern, but it didn't shield his anger.

"The lady, Iona, has a boyfriend called Tim, who knows me from work. He was supposed to have coffee with me here in Bellagio, but couldn't come on the trip at the last minute." Antonio started to explain very quickly in broken English.

I could feel the blood drain from my face. I don't know if it was anger or total shock and confusion. I had a flashback about my conversation with Tim a week before the trip. There was a work colleague who worked in the Italian branch of his firm and would be in Bellagio at the same time as us. He would like to meet for coffee, as they always talked on the phone. Antonio was the name Tim had mentioned.

"Okay, okay," I said, trying to gather my thoughts. "Tim did mention that you were meeting for coffee while we were here, but that doesn't explain why you're here, taking pictures of us with your phone. Also, why did you not say anything when you met me in the hotel bar?"

"I didn't know what to say. I wasn't supposed to meet you and Tim until Monday. I got a message from Tim. He tells me he wasn't in Bellagio, but his girlfriend was."

"Just to clarify, I'm not his girlfriend," I blurted out.

"Are you not Iona? It looks like you in the picture, " Antonio said, looking startled.

"Yes, I'm Iona, oh fuck, it's complicated. What picture? And tell us why you're on this boat creepily watching us!" I exclaimed.

I looked over at Mike, who also seemed confused.

"So, Tim tells me you're here; I told him I was in the hotel, and he told me he was supposed to be staying there. He sent me a picture of you and said to look out for you. I met you in the hotel bar, but you said you were going out. I didn't get a chance to tell you I knew who you were. Then I texted Tim to tell him you went out with Mike Maloney. He told me to keep watch and make sure you behaved!"

"Oh, for fucks sake," I shouted, too loudly. "Are you telling me he has asked you to follow me and take pictures, seriously? Also, you could've told me who you were. We talked about your brother owning a restaurant in Glasgow, and you could've said then that you knew Tim!"

"Eh, Tim was upset when he heard you had gone to dinner with Mike Maloney. So, I said I'm sure it's innocent, but he asked me to keep watch."

Mike was looking at me, then at Antonio.

"Tim is married, so maybe his wife should ask you to track Tim rather than Tim asking you to follow me! I bet he never told you that!"

Antonio gave a strange look, which made me think he already knew this.

Mike decided to step in. He had been standing on the sidelines, wanting to hear the facts first.

"This lovely lady came herself to Bellagio, Antonio. She's single and can do what she wants, move freely, and see who she chooses. You're stalking her at the moment, and I could report you to the local police for this and also for trespassing on this boat. So, here is what is going to happen. You're going to give me your phone."

Mike extended his hand, and Antonio handed him the phone. Then Mike took the phone and demanded the password. Antonio told him, under the circumstances, it wouldn't have been wise not to. Mike towered above him and looked formidable at that moment. Mike checked the phone and removed the pictures Antonio had taken of us.

"Have you told Tim anything more than seeing Iona leaving the hotel with me?" he asked.

"No," Antonio answered.

Mike removed the SIM card from the phone, destroyed it, and launched it into the lake like a pro.

"My phone!" Antonio cried out.

"That is the least of your troubles," said Mike, "I hope you're a good swimmer."

Then he started to walk towards him. I thought surely, he wasn't going to throw him overboard.

Mike grabbed Antonio by the lapels of his jacket and held him against the boat's rail.

"Don't ever pull a stunt like that again on a lady! Do you understand?"

"Yes," squealed Antonio.

"And don't send any more messages about Iona to Tim, do you understand?"

"Yes," Antonio said again.

By this point, the skipper had realised something was wrong and had appeared. Mike told the skipper to take Antonio into the cabin with him and keep him there until he was safely back in Bellagio. He gave the skipper a bundle of cash.

"Once he's off the boat, you can give him that cash to buy a new phone!"

Mike turned round and grinned at me, "You're an intriguing woman, Iona, bringing that level of drama on a date! Would you like to rekindle the night with drinks on the terrace at my villa? Or would you prefer to go back to your hotel? I know it's difficult for your lover's workmate to stalk you."

I burst out laughing. Actually, with relief, I thought this incident had killed the most romantic day and night of my life.

"I think I need a strong whisky after that, have you got a bottle in the villa?"

"Oh, I've special single malts I've been keeping until the day I met a crazy, beautiful woman from Scotland. I believe this is the day!"

I was venturing further into this amazing dream with the gorgeous Mike Maloney. We leaned on the boat's rail and looked out at the water. Neither of us spoke, both silently digesting what had just happened.

I wanted to throw my phone away. I couldn't believe Tim. My being away affected him so much that he asked someone to spy on me. This was a red flag, someone who was in too deep. I would need to set him straight in the morning about it. However, tonight it wouldn't disturb me anymore as I didn't intend to retire to my hotel room for the night. Oh no, I was ready for romantic heaven.

"A penny for them," said Mike.

"Just a penny?" I replied, laughing, "I think my thoughts just now are like gold dust!"

"Oh, tell me more," said Mike playfully.

I smiled at him, hoping I looked like a mischievous siren. You always hope you look the way you think you do when you're in these moments. I held his gaze with mine. It must have worked as he slid his hands around my waist and pulled me in close. Then I knew it had worked as I could feel how hard he was as he pressed against me. It sent all kinds of sensations right through me. This was a long, slow tease with all these interruptions.

He passionately kissed me again, and I responded the same way. It was right, it was perfect. We were so in tune.

Do you know how sometimes kissing someone is too wet or halted and can be awkward? In the past, I hadn't continued dating someone if the kissing was awful.

Good kissing was up there for me! Anyway, this kissing was five-star, triple-A rated. I couldn't get enough of it.

Chapter 12

The boat shuddered slightly, which was the cue that we were coming into dock at the private jetty beside Mike's villa.

We slowly stopped kissing, and it wasn't easy to stop. What a sight before me.

Old stone steps led up from the water to ornate gardens lit with soft lights. The villa rose from the beautiful garden in majestic white with a red roof. It was stunning.

I giggled as I made my way off the boat onto the first step, Mike holding my hand to keep me steady. I loved the warm and strong touch of his hand in mine. I still had my shoes off. The first couple of steps were wet from the lake. The freezing water splashed on my ankles, and I shrieked.

Mike looked at me, wondering what was wrong.

"I'm okay," I laughed. It was just the freezing water on my ankles; I wasn't expecting it to be cold.

"Oh, I'll soon heat you," he said confidently, staring at me.

This made me do another kind of strange, animal-type shriek. And I thought to myself, shut up, stop making animal mating noises. You know how noises come out of your mouth, and you don't know where they came from! Luckily, Mike laughed and continued to disembark.

The skipper waved us off and started to turn the boat around. Taking him and Antonio back in the direction of Bellagio.

Mike waved from the steps and shouted, "Remember, Antonio, no more spying on people!" And off we went up the stairs toward Mike's grand villa.

At the top of the stairs was a long swimming pool which ran the length of the villa. It was twinkling in the lights and looked so inviting.

As if Mike read my mind, he said, "Do you fancy a dip?"

Again, I spoke before thinking, "I've not got my bikini with me!"

Of course, I didn't have a bikini; I was out for dinner and didn't expect a midnight swim.

Mike had a wicked look in his eye. Before I knew what was happening, he was stripping off. Wow, he was so fit. I was staring at him, glued to the spot in wonder. He was stark naked, and not even Michael Angelo's "David" could compete.

Fuck it

I hauled my dress off.

He was already in, a beautiful dive. I was deliberating on whether I was keeping on my bra and knickers. I knew he had gone full monty, so, to hell with it, off they came as well.

I went to the edge of the pool. Mike was in the middle, treading water. I could see him looking at me, I would say with appreciation. I was so glad I'd been working out and hitting myself with the 40:30:30 diet. I was amazed at my confidence standing there in all my glory. How could I've known that when I got in my taxi the afternoon before, this would be my current situation one day later, acting like Lady Godiva at the side of Mike Maloney's swimming pool?

"Come on in then," Mike shouted.

I smiled at him. I deliberated whether to ease myself in or do my graceful, elegant dive. I knew I could dive pretty well, but occasionally it could go wrong. However, I felt Neptune was on my side tonight for a spectacular dive. I went in the pool with an award-winning dive, an absolute peach of a dive. My head went into the water, and I knew that was the end of the curls. The holiday hair was about to surface, but in the grand scale of this moment, I didn't care.

The water was cool but not freezing; after all the drama, it was refreshing. I came up for air, and Mike was right beside me.

"Someone is a good diver," he said, laughing, and I laughed too. I felt euphoric.

Mike could stand where we had landed in the pool, while I was a little out of my depth.

He lifted me with his arms and started to kiss me. I cuddled into his heavenly body and willingly kissed him back. He was delicious in every way. He carried me over to the pool's edge at the shallow end and sat me on it. If there was any chill in the spring Italian night sky, I didn't feel it. I was hot. Hot for this gorgeous man who was literally turning my world upside down. At that precise moment, there was only here and now. There was no one else in the world apart from the two of us and I was as horny as hell.

Mike moved in really close to me. He moved back the wisps of hair that were falling over my face. Then he looked into my eyes, and I looked back.

He kissed my lips again, more strongly. He was groaning now, and I moaned softly back. Then he was kissing my neck. He gathered my wet hair in his hand and tugged it gently. He pulled my head to the side and then kissed the nape of my neck; it was terrific. Slow and intimate.

With my hands on his sides, I pulled him nearer so I could run my fingers up and down his muscle-bound back. He was firm and solid, like a Roman god. Jupiter was in the building. He groaned, and then he was on my breasts, kissing them and probing them with his tongue. I gasped in delight.

Then his hands were down on my thighs, moving up and down and slowly massaging them. I put my hands in the water and used my thumbs to massage around his groin, getting closer slowly. Then his fingers were inside me and I was moaning loudly, it was so fucking good. I took his cock into my hand; it was hard and ready. I started to tug it gently. Mike let out a loud groan.

Then he worked his way down my body, dragging his tongue down and then into me. He knew just where to put his tongue, and I leaned back squealing in ecstasy. I was tugging faster on his gorgeous cock. I wanted to taste it. As if Mike knew this, suddenly, I was in the water. He pushed my head into the water as I took a deep breath. I was able to take his cock deep in my mouth sucking it, then dragging my lips over it. I loved having him in my mouth. I held all his energy while I pleasured him. With my air capacity exhausted, I released him. I came up for air, gasping, and Mike grabbed me, lifting me. I wrapped my legs around his waist, and he entered me. It was frantic. We were kissing, tongues in each other's mouths as he fucked me hard. It was fucking amazing. He pulled hard on my hair; I couldn't get enough of him. I wanted it to last forever. Then he sat me back up on the edge of the pool and fucked me slowly, looking right into my eyes and me into his. Time stood still, only he and I existed. Our bodies were gelled together in this slow fuck heaven. We both had our hands around the back of each other's necks. He was pulling my hair back. Then it got faster and harder as we both got ready to release all the energy built up over this crazy day.

I loved the way he was pounding into me; I responded by thrusting back. At the same time, we both exploded, crying out into the night sky. I had never felt anything like it. We were clinging to each other, our bodies shuddering in ecstasy. What a fucking ride. I fell back on the grass, and Mike managed to slide out of the pool and collapse by my side. We were breathless. Lying there on the cool grass, naked and satisfied. We smiled at each other, then he intimately kissed me while gently stroking me.

We lay there naked under the starlit sky with no care in the world. If only every night in life were like this one.

Chapter 13

"Okay, gorgeous crazy lady," Mike said, breaking the silence. "I think we need to get you the whiskey I promised you before we catch a cold!"

I wasn't feeling cold; his warm body pressed against mine was delightful and warm, however, a wee dram sounded lovely. Although I wasn't sure I wanted to let this particular moment end. I also wondered if my legs would carry me after such a magnificent shag.

Mike stood up; he was a gloriously naked man who was wonderfully in proportion. The moonlight shone on him, and I thought I was dreaming. He extended his hand to me. I took it, and he pulled me to my feet. Then cuddled me into his nakedness. Squeezing me tightly. We gelled together in this perfect embrace. Then he let me go and ran across the grass shouting, "Catch me!"

"No bother!" I thought as I took to my feet. I was a good runner; flat grass and bare feet weren't a problem. My big boobs, however, could always enjoy the support of a sports bra! He wasn't getting away from me. I ran speedily across the grass. He was surprised at how quickly I caught him. I grabbed him by the shoulders from behind.

He laughed, then scooped me up in a piggyback and carried me the rest of the way to a small wooden shed painted white. I highly recommend naked piggy bank riding on the banks of Lake Como with a hot actor. I know it isn't the easiest activity to get organised, however, look how it happened to me!

Mike opened the shed. He whipped out two luxurious hooded bathrobes. They were white and fluffy. Once I put it on, I realised I was starting to cool down. He then provided me with flip-flops.

He looked so handsome in the white bathrobe; I could have participated in round two right then.

He took my hand and led me behind the shed, and there was a gorgeous pool bar, all lit up, waiting for us. I got up on one of the bar stools and Mike poured me a McCallan 1980 Whiskey. I knew it was expensive. It was like liquid gold.

He offered me ice or a mixer, but I told him it was sacrilege if you didn't drink a single malt neat. Mike laughed, impressed that I didn't want to spoil the whiskey.

He took my hand and led me from the stool to an area with an outdoor heater in the centre of the table. There was a comfortable, cushioned garden sofa. The cushions were full and puffy. The two of us snuggled up together on the sofa and sipped our whiskey. It was blissful.

We sat there in beautiful silence. I don't always do silence well; I usually have to say something, but I didn't feel the need to speak on this occasion. You need to savour these moments like the fine whiskey we were drinking.

After a while, Mike broke the silence. "When I got up this morning, I had a feeling the day would be different."

"Oh, I thought maybe you met a different woman every Saturday in the town who got followed by a lover's colleague!" I replied.

"Yeah, every week," Mike laughed. "Are you happy to stay for the night?"

"I could be tempted," I giggled back.

"How rude of me not to have taken you into the villa yet," Mike remarked.

"Well, I was just thinking the same," I replied, "imagine not letting me get past the pool."

Then we both rolled about on the sofa laughing and started kissing again.

"I could kiss those soft lips all night," Mike whispered in my ear.

"Please do," I whispered back. I had no idea what I looked like. My hair must have been a riot, but I didn't care. In the heady heights of paradise, vanity vanishes.

Mike kissed me more, on my lips, on my cheeks, down onto my neck. The smell of whiskey on his breath was sexy.

"You're one sexy lady," he whispered. His hands started to go inside my robe, "You've got amazing tits, and they are real!" This surprised him.

Then, bold me said, "Why don't you drink your whiskey off them?"

And with the biggest grin on his face, Mike took me up on the challenge. He opened my robe and poured that expensive McCallan Whiskey over my magnificent tits and licked it off. It was so naughty, and I love that he did it. I moaned as he enjoyed every last drop of his dram.

When he hadn't lost a drop, he looked right at me and asked me where I would drink mine from. So, I shoved him back on the chair, opened his rob and I poured the most expensive Whiskey dram I had ever tasted over his marvellous big cock and licked it slowly dry.

From his groans, I could tell he was thrilled. I came up smiling with delight.

"That is how to enjoy a single malt," I laughed. But he had a wild look in his eye.

Then he pulled me on top of him and straddled me across him. I rode him like a wild horse, screaming in ecstasy. He let me free on his cock. Then suddenly he turned me over and fucked me from behind, grabbing my tits and nuzzling into the back of my neck as he took me to the heights of pleasure once more. It was rough and wild. I was amazed we had the energy in us, but once again, our bodies shuddered simultaneously in pleasure. This was the ultimate high.

I had almost forgotten we were outside. This moment captivated me. We lay naked under the stars. Mike pulled our robes over us and covered me up to ensure I was snug. He wrapped his strong arms around me and kissed my forehead. Suddenly, it was so peaceful. I was satisfied and content like never before. I allowed myself to relax into his body. For once, I felt I didn't need to speak; I could enjoy the silence because it was saying so much.

And in this adorable situation, we drifted off to sleep.

Chapter 14

The sun's rays stroked my face. I could hear the birds singing. I felt the weight of an arm around my waist. For a moment, I was confused, but then the madness of the previous day came flooding back to me. Was it real?

I looked and saw Mike's handsome face. He was still sleeping, but he looked content, like I was. It was real.

I had no idea what time it was, but by the sun's position, I reckoned it was early, about 7 am What a way to wake up on a Sunday morning in Italy on my single-lady trip! I like to expect the unexpected, but this was beyond what I could've daydreamed about!

I knew my handbag would be around the pool, and my phone was in it. However, I had no plan to retrieve it to check the time.

Mr Gorgeous and I were cuddling, so time could stand still for now. I was content to lie beside him and watch him sleep. I knew later that my boys would expect me to check in. However, they would've been partying on a Saturday night, so they wouldn't want to hear from me until the afternoon.

Then, I remembered Antonio on the boat. I had conveniently locked away the episode due to the events afterwards. Tim had asked him to spy on me. Right now, I could only begin to imagine my conversation with Tim about this. We were definitely at the end of what had been fun while it lasted. However, I didn't feel sad that it was over for Tim and me. He could get on with his life with his wife and family before he made a complete arse of his life by acting jealous with me.

Mike stirred and then opened his eyes.

"Oh, thank fuck you weren't just a dream," he grinned.

This was music to my ears.

"Oh, you're still in your dream," I teased.

And he let out a hearty laugh, then climbed on top of me and gave me the best, slow morning fuck. I did succumb to him instantly. Usually, by this point, I would like to brush my teeth and shower before getting up close and personal again. But he had taken a swig of whisky and then dribbled drips of it on my lips, and hey presto, whisky is the new toothpaste.

It was slow, it was sensational, it was out of this world. He was kissing me hard while slowly pounding into me. He pinned me down by my wrists. We both called out in pleasure, and I felt as if I was having an out-of-body experience. We collapsed apart on the sofa, naked again, in the morning sun.

Then he asked, "So what would you like to do today, then?" And we both burst out laughing.

Just at that, I was aware of a presence. I heard a slight, polite cough. Startled, I looked at Mike, but he expertly pulled the robes up and then shouted.

"Come over!"

A pristinely dressed gentleman appeared. He was the butler.

I wasn't sure what to think. Had he seen us shagging like wild animals. I could feel myself blushing.

As if Mike knew what I was thinking, he whispered, "It is okay, he always coughs like that before approaching. He is very polite."

"Lorenzo, this is Iona, she's from Scotland and is my guest here at the moment."

"I'm delighted to meet you, Iona," Lorenzo said, smiling at me warmly. Let me know at any time if you need anything, and I or the house staff will oblige."

"Thank you. It's nice to meet you," I said, smiling back.

All of a sudden, a fresh robe and slippers were laid out for Mike and me. This was fabulous.

Where would you like breakfast served this morning, Mike?" Lorenzo asked.

I loved the fact that Mike and Lorenzo were on first-name terms, none of the stuffy "Sir" nonsense.

Mike told him to serve it beside the pool, and we would be over in half an hour. Then, for the next ten minutes, he lay there kissing me gently and stroking my face.

"Okay, crazy Scottish woman," he whispered, "let's get some breakfast, I think we've worked hard for it."

"It was hard," I said, winking at Mike. And we both rolled about laughing again.

He lifted the bathrobes and slippers and led me naked over to an outhouse, which was the shower room.

Then, we went inside, and before I knew it, there was soapy lather everywhere, Mike and I were massaging soap into each other, and he washed my hair. Seriously, he washed my hair. My hair would be a riot as I had no straighteners with me. Who was this new me who didn't care about her holiday hair?

We then wrapped each other in giant bath towels and dried off.

Mike then presented me with a cupboard with a hairdryer, a full range of hair products, and GHD straighteners.

Mike explained to me that he sometimes held summer garden and pool parties. He also allowed movie makers and magazines to use the villa as a film location and for model shoots. His housekeeper suggested that all the merchandise and products left behind would be handy for any guests to get ready after being in the pool.

"Well, your housekeeper is correct," I said, laughing happily as I blow-dried my hair. Mike sat watching me. He seemed enthralled with the effort I put into getting my hair dried.

Then I expertly created wispy curls with the straighteners. I was so pleased he had these facilities. You all know what I'm talking about; getting ready properly is the best.

We put on the luxurious bath robes and approached the pool terrace.

Chapter 15

It was beautiful in the daytime. The gorgeous gardens were arrayed with spring flowers in multiple colours. The lakeside and mountains looked splendid. What a view. The table was set for two. There was a selection of hams, cheese, eggs, fruit, bread, and a pot of coffee. I could smell the coffee long before we reached the table. There was also freshly squeezed orange juice.

"Is there anything you want to request specifically?" Mike asked.

"I think I'll be fine with this feast," I laughed.

He grinned and pulled out my chair for me. He kissed me on the forehead as I sat down, before sitting across from me and grinning. His smile was so infectious that I had to smile back. Then we realised how hungry we were.

Like a pair of wolves, we tore into the feast before us. Like a hungry wolf, I ripped a giant piece of bread off the loaf. Then I saw there was a bread knife on the table. I was pleased to see Mike didn't sue the knife either. Sometimes you can be too primal and hungry for etiquette.

I loaded the bread with butter and cheese and devoured it. I tried to do it ladylike, but you know what it's like: When there is butter, cheese, and crusty bread, it gets messy. I had put a napkin over me before I started, so at least it caught the crumbs. Then, onto the fruit. Mike and I sat there eating for about ten minutes. There was no conversation. Then again, we laughed.

"You would think we had used up lots of energy or something," I giggled.

Mike reached across the table and took my hand. We just looked at each other, smiling. He then offered me black grapes, and I said,

"Oh, you could lie down, and I could feed them to you as if you're Julius Caesar!"

Mike laughed as if it were the funniest thing he had ever heard.

We finished our food and then properly drank coffee from a cup and saucer on this gorgeous Italian spring morning. The sun was glistening on Lake Como, the birds were singing, and my heart was singing. I was floating in a bubble, and I didn't want this bubble to burst.

After a while, we looked over at each other.

"Okay, Mike said, did you have any plans for today?"

"No," I replied, "I was just going to meander through the town and see how my day unfolded."

"Would you like to spend it with me?" he grinned.

"Okay!" I agreed far too eagerly.

Mike smiled broadly.

We made plans. Mike asked Lorenzo to arrange a picnic basket in the kitchen. We were going to sail back to Bellagio first so I could get a change of clothes. Then Mike asked me if I wanted to borrow his daughter's clothes instead. She was in her twenties and about my size. He reassured me she wouldn't mind; she just kept a clothes wardrobe here for when she visited.

This seemed like a plan, as there was no other particular need for me to return to my hotel. Getting back there would've taken up part of the day.

I hadn't even been inside Mike's villa yet. I gasped as Lorenzo led us up the marble stairs and through the large glass doors that looked out to the pool. We were in a giant atrium with white marble tiles leading to a grand staircase. A chandelier hung above the stairs. I could see that rooms leading off the atrium were all decorated to the highest standards. All in warm neutrals. It was so tasteful and expensive. I had to pinch myself. Although I had already been in Mike's company and on his boat, it was only dawning on me how wealthy he was. He was in another league, a different world from my reality, even with my smart investments.

However, I wouldn't start acting shy and intimidated by this, as I hadn't seen any arrogance from him about how rich he was or any signs of grandeur.

"You go on with Lorenzo, Iona, and I'll see you back down here when you're ready," Mike grinned and wandered off toward one of the downstairs lounges.

Loranzo took me up the grand staircase to a long gallery that looked as if it went on forever. It was sparkling white marble and had excellent lighting. I had a thing about light; I always thought light could create or ruin a room or an atmosphere. This light was excellent, the morning light streaming in from large glass windows. Standing in the gallery, you can see the downstairs atrium and right out to the pool.

Lorenzo stopped at three doors along the gallery. He opened the giant white door that led into a beautiful bedroom. A big plush rug covered the floor in front of a massive bed. Luxurious bedding adorned the bed, which looked like you shouldn't touch it. It was picture perfect; the temptation to lie on it was real, but I didn't.

Lorenzo pulled back a folding door, and a giant walk-in closet was before me. I was in awe. If you had seen my wardrobe back home and how untidy it was, you would understand why I was in awe.

It was a perfectly managed clothes space. There was no Primark here; it was all designer brands: Gucci, Versace, Valentino. I hoped it would fit me, especially after eating all that cheese and bread for breakfast.

"Help yourself, Iona, I'll leave you in peace to select what you want. Just press this button if you need help or want me to show you the way back downstairs."

"Thank you, Lorenzo," I replied, trying not to sound too excited about this closet.

Lorenzo left, and I stared all around me. What to wear! All Mike had said was to dress for walking and sit for a picnic.

I saw a gorgeous baby blue Versace summer dress with thin straps. I loved this colour on me. Lorenzo had carefully collected my clothes from around the pool and put them in the room for me. So, I had my bra. I also noticed brand new knickers in the closet, label still on. So, I had my bra and clean knickers. I pulled on my underwear and carefully pulled the dress over my head. I couldn't believe it was a perfect fit. Why was everything happening like an ideal dream?

I decided that for footwear, I would put on trainers. Here was a perfect pair of white Gucci trainers. I noticed there were brand-new trainer socks in the drawer too. So, I put them on and laced up my trainers. I felt like a million dollars.

Lorenzo had also fetched my handbag, so I had my makeup. I looked at my phone, but the battery was dead. I was happy with this as I knew there would be loads of messages from Tim. I knew my boys wouldn't expect to hear from me until late afternoon. Therefore, I decided not to charge it and spoil this amazing time by having to read Tim's messages. I was delaying that for later.

I fixed my makeup—not too much, just a natural glow. There was a dressing table in the closet full of fantastic cosmetics, so I'll not pretend I did apply the blusher. I noticed a bottle of Creed, Jardin d'Amalfi Parfum sitting there. The bottle was open, so I sprayed it!

I had already fixed my hair at the pool earlier, so I was ready.

I didn't think I needed Lorenzo to show me the way back down the stairs. I went out into the hallway to the top of the staircase.

Mike was standing at the bottom, smiling up at me.

"Wow, you look amazing," he said.

My legs turned to jelly. He stood there wearing the crispest white T-shirt I had ever seen, followed by cream cargo shorts and trainers. He looked amazing.

There was a marble banister going right down the staircase.

My mouth spoke before I thought about what I was going to say.

"I've always wanted to slide down one of these big banisters," I heard myself say.

Mike's face looked like a picture, then he replied, "Well, what is stopping you?"

"Oh, is that a dare?" I teased.

"Come on!" Mike encouraged, "I'll catch you."

And there he stood at the bottom of the banister, arms outstretched. How could I resist?

I put down my handbag and straddled the banister. I looked at the drop on the other side. It wasn't so high. If necessary, I could fall graciously onto the stairs. I was flashing my knickers at Mike, but I wasn't in the mood to give a damn. I slid down, keeping my balance and giggling as I went. It was fast as the marble was slippery.

Before I knew it, Mike was scooping me up in his arms at the bottom and laughing hard.

"You're crazy, Iona. I love it!" he laughed and gently lowered me to a standing position. Then we laughed and laughed until tears ran down our cheeks.

When we stopped laughing, we hugged each other warmly. Then Mike ran up the stairs to fetch my handbag, which I had left at the top.

"Right," said Mike, "let's get on the boat before I take you right back up the stairs."

I ran in front of him,

"Only if you can catch me!"

He chased me out and down the steps towards the jetty. I was squealing as he chased me around the side of the pool towards the boat. It was ridiculous, silly behaviour, and I felt alive.

Just as I reached the jetty steps, he caught me. Then he tickled me, and I laughed hysterically. I almost peed myself.

"Stop, stop," I squealed. Then he just gave me a big, intense, full-on kiss on the mouth.

"Right, lady," he said masterfully, "get on that boat, now."

I turned to go on the boat, and he cheekily slapped my arse. I've to say I liked it. Usually, if someone had slapped my arse I would've turned round and punched them, but I wasn't punching this handsome face!

We went up onto the deck. The same skipper as last night greeted us warmly.

Chapter 16

"So, where are we going?" I asked, and then I thought I didn't know my location at the moment. Last night we came across the lake on the boat. I had no bloody clue where I was. It's incredible how something like that should be concerning, but at that moment, it wasn't.

"In fact," I said, "where are we right now?"

Mike looked at me and said, "I forgot you don't know where you are." Then with a wicked grin, he said, "So, I could keep you here forever."

"Oh, don't tempt me!" I said right back at him.

Then we laughed more. I just kept laughing with this guy. My endorphin production was on overdrive.

"At the moment you're in the area of Laglio," Mike said, looking more serious. "I will take you to a little island called Isola Comacina. It's right in the middle of the lake."

"Oh, we'll be able to play hide and seek then!" I blurted out.

"Oh yeah," smiled Mike, "but I'll find you!"

I didn't want to hide from him anyway, and I would definitely want him to find me.

The Lake was gorgeous on this glorious Sunday morning. You could see tourist boats dotted about. People were on their holidays, enjoying the scenery, but I could bet they weren't having as much fun as I was, at that precise moment in time.

Mike sat beside me with his arm around my shoulder. We were enjoying the scenery. A contented peacefulness. I couldn't believe that we hadn't met this time yesterday.

The boat cut through the water, and Mike pointed out the landmarks to me. Up in the distance on the right was Bellagio, where it had all begun in the café.

Then Mike pointed to the left, and I could see a gorgeous, green, wooded island perched beautifully in the middle of the water. From what I could see, there were buildings scattered around the island.

"What are the buildings?" I asked.

"There are a few restaurants on there," he replied. "There is also a church from Roman times."

"Oh, that would be such a nice place to get married," I thought aloud. Then I blushed, I hope he didn't know I was a nutter who had just met him and wanted a wedding. (Although it wasn't the worst thought I had ever had.)

"Oh, we can have our wedding there," Mike laughed, and I laughed right back at him.

We were at a jetty, and the boat was lined up. Mike put on a baseball cap and sunglasses.

"I can't be bothered getting recognised today, I just want us to have fun," he told me.

It wouldn't have mattered what he did. He was hot.

He extended his hand to help me off the boat. There was that electric spark. Every time I touched him, I felt wired to a source.

The skipper was offloading a delightful picnic hamper—the nice wicker kind with plates and champagne flutes inside. I knew there would be a choice of delicious food in there, too. Mike was giving the skipper directions, and off he went with the picnic hamper and another bag.

"I've sent the cavalry ahead," said Mike. "We will go the scenic route to our picnic.

He took my hand and led me along a path. This place was of such natural beauty. Surrounded by Olive, Linden, and Laurel trees, it was beautiful. There were stunning views of the villages and towns around Lake Como.

Mike and I wandered along the path, immersed in the loveliness. We would stop every so often and look out at the Lake. We were meandering through the island, and we started talking about how we loved walking in the woods as children. His stories of woodland life in the USA and mine of Scottish forests are different experiences in terms of landscape and wildlife, but they are the same experience from a child's adventurous mind.

We must have walked for about an hour without realising. Then he led me to where he had sent the skipper in advance.

In a clearing, there was a giant picnic mat laid out with the hamper sitting on it. There was a bottle of champagne cooling in a cooler. Rays from the sun shone down onto the clearing. It was so picturesque. There was no sign of the skipper.

Mike must have seen me looking for him. "He is way back to the boat. We have this place to ourselves," he said, winking at me.

I giggled. After the big breakfast this morning, I was surprised how hungry I felt.

Mike opened the hamper and laid out two plates. Then he opened the boxes with the food in them: chicken breast, pasta, a colourful salad, and crusty bread. He poured me a glass of champagne, and we sat on the mat, sipping the champagne and smiling at each other.

We sat there eating our delicious food and drink with no care in the world. It felt like there were only the two of us on the planet. It was peaceful—no traffic, no people, only the birds singing.

Once Mike had finished, he lay on his back, and I lay beside him. We lay quietly, letting our food digest, breathing in the nature and the peacefulness. It was meditative.

Then we held hands. He was playing with my hand, feeling my fingers, and circling my palm with his thumb. I turned on my side to move towards him. At the same time, he turned to face me. Our eyes locked, intently gazing into each other's eyes. I was hypnotised; I could have let him hold me in that gaze for eternity.

Then we were kissing. Very gently, very intimate. He was stroking my hair.

"You're so beautiful," he was saying. "I've never met anyone like you."

His words were dropping warmly in my mind. I felt thrilled hearing him say this.

I wanted to speak but didn't want to waste it with a cliché response.

I kissed his lips. "I'm so happy right now being right here with you." I heard myself saying.

The kissing got stronger and wilder, and our passion surfaced like a wild animal. We were on an island, in an idyllic setting. In the middle of an Italian Lake. I tugged at Mike's t-shirt. I wanted to feel his body, his skin. It came loose from his shorts. He had his hand up my dress, massaging my thighs. My hands wandered over his torso, round to his side. I wanted his shirt off him. I frantically pulled it up and went down to kiss his body. He groaned. I moaned softly. Then he stood up and pulled me up. He whipped my dress right off over my head. I didn't care. Next, he loosened my bra, and my tits happily came out to play in the Italian sunshine.

He hauled off his t-shirt. Next, he just grasped at my knickers, and they were at my ankles. I stepped out of them.

There I was, completely naked outside, in the daylight, in plain sight. I didn't give a damn. I felt like a Roman goddess who would've wandered the woods like this.

Mike looked at me. Then he pushed me down onto my knees in front of him. I looked up at him, holding his gaze. Then I took the waist of his boxers with my teeth and pulled at them. Next, I put my hands up and pulled them down and his gorgeous cock came out to join me. He was so hard. I looked up at him again. He was watching, willing me to take it.

I kept my lips hovering over the top of his cock giving it teasing gentle kisses. Then my tongue started to lick it slowly. All the time I was looking up at him and staying connected with his eyes. He groaned. I knew he was loving this.

Then I started to take him into my mouth. So slowly, so teasingly.

When he knew he could take no more, Mike pulled my hair back and stopped me. Then scooped me up and carried me to the nearest tree. His eyes were wild. He held me against the tree and fucked me. In the open air, we were wild, acting out our natural urges. I thought I had died and gone to heaven. It was so good I cried out, as did he. Then we stood there, trembling in each other's arms for a considerable time. Unable to let go.

Eventually, we released each other, the sweat pouring from our bodies.

"I'm so hot," I managed to whisper.

"You are," whispered Mike, then he winked at me.

He took my hand, and we shakily returned to the picnic spot. He squeezed a giant bottle of water so that the water hit me. I shrieked at the freezing water and then grabbed a bottle myself. We had a tremendous water fight, which cooled us down. As Sunday afternoons go, this was up there with the best.

It was time to head back to the boat. I didn't want this day to end, but I knew it would. Mike and I walked back through the trees toward the boat. However, just before we got there, the skipper urgently approached us. His face told me there was something wrong.

"We have trouble!" he said, looking at Mike. "The police are waiting at Bellagio, at the harbour, to speak to all of us. I've just received word on the radio. They won't say what it's about."

"All of us?" Mike asked. "They want to see all of us?"

The skipper nodded as he took the picnic basket off Mike and ushered us towards the boat.

My head was spinning. Why did the Bellagio police want to speak to us?

"What can this be about?" I voiced aloud. I suddenly felt panicked. I'd spent the last 24 hours with a guy I had just met. There had been a stalker on the boat, and now the police wanted to speak to us.

"Was there any issue with that guy, Antonio, when you dropped him off?" Mike asked the skipper.

He shook his head. No, he got off moaning about not having his phone. However, he was happy when I gave him the money you provided to replace it. There wasn't any disturbance.

We all got on the boat, unsure of the mystery waiting for us at Bellagio.

It was as if someone had taken a pin and burst our bubble. I shivered.

Mike put his arm around me, and I felt guilty that I was panicking. He was warm and kind.

"I'm sure it will be something over nothing!" he said.

I put my head on his shoulder, and we sat silently as the boat made its way back across Lake Como to Bellagio. It would be a thirty-minute crossing, so we would need to be patient and find out what had happened.

It was a long thirty minutes. As we made our way to Bellagio, I realised this dream I'd been in for the last 24 hours couldn't last forever. The reality of life would steal us back from this blissful time. Mike and I couldn't remain glued together like the only two people in the world. It is stunning how meeting a particular person could change your life and grab your heart so quickly. In such a way, the rest of your world paled into insignificance.

Mike kissed my forehead, nuzzling into it. I looked round and gazed into his eyes. He knew it, too; we had been living a fairytale, and now it looked like trouble was ahead.

If I had the choice to sit on the boat with Mike forever, I would've taken it.

Chapter 17

We were approaching the harbour, and it was clear to see a commotion going on: two police cars, an ambulance, a crowd of people, and someone waving frantically.

I felt the colour drain from my face.

What the hell?

I really couldn't believe it. It was Tim. Tim was waving frantically.

Why was he here?

What had happened?

Then rage gathered in me, why the fuck was he here and what was going on?

"Iona, Iona," he was roaring my name from the Jetty.

"No need to guess who that is," Mike said. I couldn't tell if there was annoyance in his voice, but he certainly didn't sound happy.

My heart sank into the pit of my stomach. I knew good things ended, but this was painful. I had landed on planet Earth from the dizzy heights Mike took me to.

"Ioan, Iona," Tim shouted, "thank goodness you're okay."

I was near enough now to see his face. It was a contorted look of worry and joy.

I then looked at Mike, and he looked back at me. We were equally confused by this situation. What was going on?

"Are you okay?" Mike asked me.

"I don't know, I'm so confused with all this, Mike, I wish we had stayed on the island."

Mike gave me a big grin. " So, the hell do I?" he laughed. Come on, let's get this sorted."

The comfort of his words, his hands still on my back, ensured I was fine. This calmed my soul.

The skipper had anchored the boat and put out the gangplank to disembark. Mike went up first and turned to give me a hand. A uniformed police officer was waiting at the end of the plank. Tim was jumping up and down behind him like a lively puppy. Another officer came behind Tim and put his hand on his shoulder, as if to calm him down.

"Mr Mike Maloney?" a suited gentleman appeared. Mike nodded. "I'm Ispettore (*translation: Inspector*) Gustavo Colombo. I would like you to accompany me to the police station to discuss a kidnapping and an attempted murder."

Mike and I looked at each other in disbelief. Kidnapped? Who? And who was the victim of the attempted Murder?

I was trying to speak, but words weren't coming out of my mouth. At this point, Tim escaped from the police officer holding him back.

It happened suddenly; he came charging towards Mike, who was standing on dry land.

"You better not have hurt her," Tim screamed at Mike. Before Mike could answer, Tim lunged forward and shoved Mike so forcibly that he lost his balance. In slow motion, Ispettore Colombo reached out to grab Mike, but it was too late. Mike fell backwards into the water. He must have grabbed Tim's shirt as he fell in with him.

I knew Mike could swim, as I had seen him in the pool in the dreamy haze of the early morning. However, I knew Tim couldn't swim. As much as I wanted to punch his lights out for this fiasco, he had a child and needed to be saved.

I threw off my shoes and jumped in.

I didn't expect the lake to be so cold, so it initially took my breath away. As I came to the surface, I could see Mike. He was holding

Tim afloat, but Tim was still trying to get a punch in.

The silly bastard couldn't swim, and he was trying to fight with a guy who was keeping him from drowning!

"Tim," I shouted, "calm the fuck down! He is trying to fucking save you here. You can't fucking swim!"

"Tim looked round at me. "He kidnapped you; I'm not going to let him off with that!"

I was now treading water with this information.

"Tim, who has fucking kidnapped me? Do I look like a kidnappee?"

"You were missing for overnight, not answering your phone. What was I supposed to think?" Tim shouted at me. "That is no way to treat someone you're supposed to care about!"

Even though my thoughts were about not wanting to be with him anymore, I felt sorry. I just escaped into a magic twenty-four-hour fantasy and let the rest of the world go to hell.

"Right, we need to talk this through, but not in here," I said, calmer. Treading water and thinking, I couldn't believe this was happening.

"I couldn't agree more," said Mike. "He looked over at me with a concerned look. I wanted his twinkle in his eye look. The look he gave me made my heart sink.

The police dispatched a dinghy to rescue us from the water. Before long, we were on dry land with towels wrapped around us and a hot coffee.

I wanted to know what chain of events had happened on dry land while I was blissfully unaware in paradise. Mike was talking to Ispettore Colombo. I wanted to know about the attempted murder accusations. That was shocking. My alleged kidnapping was easily explainable, as no one had kidnapped me. However, attempted murder was worrying.

Then I looked around and saw my two sons staring at me.

I tried to speak, but no words came out. I could see my boys before me, but couldn't put the jigsaw together. Tim was here, but my boys were here, and my boys didn't know Tim.

"Mum!" Jack exclaimed, "We thought you were dead!" He was white-faced, shaking, and moving towards me. Within seconds, my two boys were hugging me as if it hadn't only been 48 hours since I last saw them.

"Dead," I asked, "why did you think I was dead?"

"He told us you might be!" Dan said, pointing to Tim.

I looked over at Tim, who looked like a wet weekend. His hair was dripping wet over his eyes, and he looked sorry for himself.

I felt rage well up in me. Why had Tim traumatised my boys with news of my apparent death?

"Tim," I yelled over. However, Ispettore Colombo got in front of me.

"We will go to the station. We need to find out what happened. Can you please come with me?"

I didn't want to go to the station. Suddenly, I felt exhausted, wet, and confused. I heard the boys saying they were coming too, and he nodded his head to them.

The police escorted my boys and me into a waiting police car. I could see Mike and the skipper getting into a car further up the road. Then I gasped when I saw Tim getting into the same car. I could only stop my imagination from running wild with how that conversation would go. I was still reeling from the concerned look Mike had given me when we were all in the water.

I rested my head back on the headrest in the back of the car. I was in the middle, with Jack and Dan on either side, each clinging to my arms.

What the hell had I done?

The boys hadn't acted like this since they were five and three.

"Ok," I managed to say, "I need to know what has happened. Tell me how you ended up gatecrashing my weekend in Bellagio just because I brought the hair straighteners with me?"

This managed to raise a laugh.

"Well," started Jack, "we had a party last night and it was about four in the morning. I was playing the guitar in the kitchen, and Milly, you know Milly, she was singing. The guys in the living room were playing dance tunes, and Dan had made pizza."

Jack loved to tell a story. It took him ages to get to the point.

"So, while Milly and I were singing, there was a knock at the door. And I'm thinking, oh no, it must be Mr McKay from next door coming to moan about the music. So, I tell Milly to answer and say she's housesitting, and she will turn the volume down. This would save me from having to have a gross conversation with him about his cabbages."

The three of us laughed at this, Mr McKay, and his bloody cabbages.

"Anyway," Jack continued, "Milly goes to the door to sort this, but she's yelling for me to come. I'm thinking, oh no, Mr McKay knows I'm here now. I get to the door and see this guy standing there. I've no idea who he is. He introduced himself as Tim; he said he was your friend, Mum. Then he tells me he thinks you might be in danger or even dead. I'm like, what the fuck."

I felt sick, my poor boys getting information like that in the middle of the night. Thank goodness Tim had introduced himself as a friend, at least not as my lover.

"So, I can't believe what he's saying," said Jack, "then I start yelling the party is over and have to extract Dan from a random girl he's kissing on the sofa."

"Eh, I know her," interrupted Dan, "she isn't random! So, mum when Jack started having a meltdown, I'm like what the shit is going down here. I see the guy, Tim, standing in our kitchen, as white as a sheet. I don't know how, but I felt you were okay. I just got a feeling you were fine."

I smiled. Dan was always calm, and Jack was dramatic.

"I told Tim to sit on a chair because I thought he might collapse otherwise," Dan continued. I said, "Right, mate, you're going to have to explain what is happening here. We don't even know you, and we've never heard of you."

I gulped, waiting for what was coming next. I keep forgetting my oldest son has a law degree and isn't a child anymore!

"What did he say?" I asked, although it sounded like a squeak.

"Well, mum, the first thing is, he said he was your boyfriend, which surprised us as we didn't know you had a boyfriend?" Dan said questioningly, looking straight at me.

"Oh..."

"So, I told him, I don't think my mum has a boyfriend, mate. He told me you probably hadn't mentioned him, as the circumstances were complicated."

"Oh..."

"I wasn't letting him off with this, as he was trying to tell us something might have happened to you. So, I asked him outright if he had done something to you. By this point, all our mates at the party gathered to listen in."

"Oh..."

"Then, he starts to cry. He tells us he has been having an affair with you. For fucks sake mum, I nearly collapsed and the whole gang gathered round were all like, astounded!"

"Shit," I thought, "Tim outed me to my boys and all their pals, what a dick!"

I was about to say something; I'm not sure what, but Dan kept talking, and Jack nodded his head.

"Don't get me wrong, mum, I still can't believe you've been having an affair; however, knowing you're alive is much more important!"

"Well thank fuck for that," I thought, then I laughed aloud at my son's reasoning.

Then, they both looked serious again and gave me a strict look.

"I had to hold myself back from punching his face for having an affair with my mother," Dan quipped.

Yes, Dan was to have a go at him," Jack said, "but the random girl pulled him back and told him we had to hear what happened."

I was thinking I liked the sound of this random girl.

"She isn't fucking random," protested Dan, "her name is Lexie! Anyway, I told Tim he had better start from the beginning. By this, I meant why he thought you were in danger or dead, but no, he goes right back to when you first met, and I can't unhear what he was saying. I managed to stop him from saying too much, but by this point, our friends in the kitchen had the popcorn out!"

I blushed. What the hell did Tim tell them about our first meeting? This was a nightmare.

"He then told us he was supposed to be going with you to Bellagio but had to call off at the last minute due to his daughter injuring herself. For fucks sake mum, he has a daughter!"

I felt like the child and the parents were scolding me. I just shrugged my shoulders. I always knew it would be awful if this had ever come out.

"Then, I turned to Jack and asked him who you were away with to Bellagio. He didn't know, and neither did I. Tim said you had gone yourself. I was thinking, no, mum would've gone with friends. I'm sorry, Mum, I realised we were too busy with our lives to notice you had gone alone."

This shocked me. I was fine going on my own, but Dan had remarked on their indifference to me going away, which I found sweet.

"Here we were," Dan continued, "with no idea where our Mum was and a random stranger imparting dreadful news. However, Tim knew the hotel you were staying at, as you were supposed to be staying there with him. He then tells us he had been trying to call you for hours, and you hadn't answered your phone. He sent text messages, and there was no response."

"I told him I had spoken to you in the afternoon, and you were fine then," Jack said.

"Tim then told us, you had met a guy he knew from work, who you would've been meeting up with for a coffee on Monday, if you had both been in Bellagio together."

I knew what was coming next.

"He had called Tim and said you looked like a supermodel in a white dress. Then the actor Mike Maloney appeared and took you to dinner. We were telling Tim, mate, your friend in Italy was talking to the wrong person, our mum wouldn't have been on a date with a Hollywood actor!"

Thanks for the confidence in your mother's ability to pull a Hollywood actor.

"Then he pulls out his phone and shows us the picture. There you were, mum, all glammed up and with Mike Maloney. The girls at the party were all trying to grab the phone to see. Now, your street cred is up high back home! They were all screeching and excited."

I burst out laughing at my street cred!

"So, there we were with Tim, our mother's lover, who is married, and she's cheating on him with a Hollywood Actor. We were thinking, have we drunk homemade vodka or something? Is this for real?"

"Tim then tells us his man on the ground in Bellagio followed you to a mountain restaurant. Then he showed us pictures of you snogging Mike Maloney, which his friend sent him. This was way too much information for us, but the girls at the party thought they were watching an episode of Love Island. However, the last he heard from the man was that he was following you to a jetty and you were getting on a boat. No contact from you or the man on the ground, since!"

It all added up, about the time Tim would've gone to my house to see my boys, Antonio's phone would've been at the bottom of Lake Como. I hadn't texted Tim since before dinner the night before.

"I said to him," Dan proceeded, "I know we have not heard from my Mum since yesterday afternoon, but why do you think she's dead or in danger? Mum has found herself a Hollywood actor, and it doesn't look like anyone is forcing her or that she's in danger in any photographs. Mum, you were having the time of your life by the look of it!"

Well, Dan wasn't wrong about that!

"Tim then explained he had called Antonio's wife. She hadn't heard from him in hours and was worried about him. Then she did "Find My iPhone" for his phone. The last known location for the iPhone was in the middle of Lake Como. So, his wife was phoning the local police. Tim said you were totally off the grid, and he was worried something had happened in the middle of Lake Como. We became worried and started calling your phone, but it went straight to voicemail. We then realised we didn't even have Find My iPhone on for you. We called the hotel, but you hadn't returned. So, with all this in mind, we decided to book flights and get here as soon as possible."

"Antonio is the name of the missing guy, and he's still missing. Someone saw him getting on the boat you were on. This was his last sighting."

I sat in silence, considering all this. I did understand why they were so worried. The last time I saw Antonio was when we got off the boat at the jetty, at Mike's house. He was alive and well then. However, I had no idea what Mike said to the Skipper, or what happened when they returned to Bellagio.

We were approaching the police station.

"I'm sorry about all of this. I hate the fact that you've both been worried. I last saw Antonio on the boat when we disembarked at Mike's villa, across the lake. I hope he's okay."

"Oh, just one more thing, Mum, we did call Dad, and he's on his way!"

As we approached the police station, I saw my ex-husband, Keith, glaring at me from the roadside.

Chapter 18

If there was one person I didn't need in this mix, it was my ex-husband. He was a good father to the boys but a pain in the arse for me. I hoped his wife wasn't with him, as that would be a double whammy. I understand why the boys involved their dad; however, I could have done without his presence.

He always had to be right, and everything was black and white. I couldn't see his wife, Sandra, anywhere, which was unusual as she never let him go far without accompanying him.

I took a deep breath and stepped out of the car. I could see Mike getting out of the vehicle further up, and Tim coming out behind them. What the hell would they have been talking about on the journey here?

Keith, my ex, marched up to me.

"What the hell are you playing at, Iona? The boys are bloody traumatised."

I looked at him. I knew he was correct, but he and I could never be on the same side. He was excruciatingly annoying.

"I understand why you've come here to support the boys, Keith, but please hear everything firsthand before flying off the handle like you usually do!"

"Flying off the handle, are you bloody serious! A strange guy tells your boys he's having an affair with you, and you're missing in Italy, presumed dead. And I've nothing to say. This is a disgrace, Iona!"

I saw Mike approaching with the detective and Tim plodding behind. It occurred to me that I must look like a wreck, as jumping in the water at the harbour left me soaking wet.

"Well, Keith," I started, "as usual, you paint the worst picture of everything."

Then I heard the shrill of his wife Sandra's voice. She was with the boys, fussing about them. I knew she had to be here somewhere.

I felt weak. All this drama, and there was a possibility that Antonio was dead. It was a horrible situation. Plus, with the addition of my ex and his wife, it was a horror story.

"You're a class act, Iona," Keith said.

Mike had now reached the same level with us.

"Who's this?" he asked.

"I'm her ex-husband, mate," Keith jumped in before I could say anything. "I got a lucky escape."

I was mad.

"Keith shut up; you're an absolute arsehole! You came here for the boys, so go and help them with your silly wife and leave me alone!"

Mike looked surprised at my outburst. I hadn't spoken to him in detail about my ex over the last day. We didn't get on, and he wasn't someone I particularly wanted to talk to.

I never expected what came next. Mike wrapped his arms around me and gave me a massive hug. It was lovely. Back at the harbour, I thought he seemed annoyed or concerned that perhaps I hadn't told him the extent of my relationship with Tim. I had. However, I would understand if Mike thought otherwise, considering Tim's lengths to try to follow my movements.

His hug, touch, and strength gave me energy. I could feel it heating my soul. I wished somebody could spirit us away from this dreadful drama we now found ourselves in. However, I would take my boys with me too!

The detective coughed, and Mike and I parted. It was time to go inside the police station and give our recollections of events.

I turned to go in. I saw the girl with her arm in a sling heading toward me. A woman in her thirties with dark hair, holding her other hand. The woman dropped the girl's hand.

I heard Tim shout,

"JESS, WHAT ARE YOU DOING HERE?"

Just as the woman punched me between the eyes, everything went black.

Chapter 19

I could hear voices; they were familiar, and I could sense a bright light. It felt like the sun.

"Is she okay?"

"Is her head bleeding?"

"Iona! Iona!"

"Mum, can you hear us?"

Then I felt the throb on the back of my head and the top of my nose. I didn't want to open my eyes. I was confused; I knew there was too much to deal with if I opened my eyes. It was coming back to me. Everyone was here. The police. My family. There was a missing person. And then, the woman who punched me, with a sinking feeling, I realised who she was.

"She's a bitch, I hate her, she deserved that!"

A woman's voice, and it was angry.

I opened my eyes.

A sea of faces looking down at me. Jack, Dan, Keith, Sandra, Tim. I could then hear a woman crying in the background. No doubt Tim's wife.

Here I was, lying on the pavement in Italy, all my secrets laid bare, the ex-wife had found out, my ex-husband was on the scene, and my boys were traumatised. I searched for Mike's face but couldn't see him. My 24 hours in paradise had turned into Bedlam in Bellagio.

"Let me through," I heard Mike saying.

His handsome face appeared in my vision. "Tim," he said authoritatively, "I think you need to go and speak to your wife!"

Just then, a paramedic appeared with a stretcher. I started to protest, saying I was okay, but they had me in a neck brace and on the stretcher. I was too weak to protest.

"We need to get you checked out!" said Ispettore Colombo, who had suddenly appeared.

Chapter 20

The next few hours were confusing. An ambulance arrived. I vomited. I didn't think it was a concussion; I think I was ill with the events that had unfolded. I felt my life spinning out of control before me.

After a thorough check, the medics said I was going to the hospital for an X-ray to check that I hadn't fractured my skull. I was rambling when I thought I was talking perfect sense. I tried to protest, but my squeaks were futile. Tied to the stretcher with my head in a brace so I couldn't move it.

Then things got even worse. Mike and Tim had to stay at the police station for questioning. My boys needed to stay too, as Tim had approached them to say I was missing, so the police wanted to know everything from start to finish. So, who did that leave to go with me to the hospital? Yes, my bloody pain in the arse of an ex-husband, Keith.

There was a reason we weren't together, as we were opposites in the universe. The initial attraction between us had worn off quickly once we married. Living in the same house with one another was torture. We couldn't stand each other; we didn't do anything bad to one another apart from constantly arguing and disagreeing.

However, I don't think I need to like him or ever be in his company apart from dealing with matters for the boys. Now that the boys were adults, I saw much less of him. Then add Sandra to the mix, his equally neurotic wife and you've the perfect pair of arseholes, a match made in hell.

So, I decided to lie there and pretend to be unconscious. That didn't work as the paramedics were slapping me and nipping me to stay awake. They were doing their job to ensure I hadn't left this earth.

Keith and Sandra were both staring at me.

"That poor woman," said Sandra. Only for an instance did I think she was referring to me; of course, she was talking about Jess, Tim's wife.

"Imagine, finding out your husband was having an affair," she continued.

Then Keith added, "Yes, and imagine finding out like this."

"Then there are our boys, knowing their mother was the one who caused the poor woman's heartache!" Sandra added.

She always referred to our boys, which irritated me. However, I regretfully had to admit she was nice to them, so it was bittersweet.

"I'm here, you know," I reminded them.

"What possessed you, Iona, to have an affair? Couldn't you just have found a single person?"

"Oh yeah, Keith, it's that straightforward, when it comes to sex, drugs, and rock'n'roll," I retorted, knowing this would irritate him.

"Oh, here she goes," stated Sandra.

"Yes, here she goes," repeated Keith.

I laughed sarcastically. "Here you two fucking go!"

They both put on their offended, shocked, or disapproving faces. They used this expression often in my company, even though they weren't in my company that often.

"Wait a minute," Keith started. We were having a charming weekend, then in the early hours of this morning, I got a call from the boys telling me you might be dead. So, we came here to support them and discover all sorts of shocking things, and so do they! This is your doing, Iona!"

Well, when he put it like that, but he was in school principal mode, and I really couldn't be arsed at this point with being the schoolchild. My head hurt; my mind hurt. Fuck, what a mess.

I let out a huge sigh. The paramedic motioned to Keith and Sandra, putting his finger up to his mouth, to signal them to stop talking. What a guy, you know how you can instantly like someone. The two of them instantly shut up and did what they were told. This was bliss for me at this stage.

When we arrived at the hospital, they wheeled me to a room and transferred me to a bed. I saw Keith and Sandra stopping at the desk, enjoying being the ones to give all my details in an official capacity. They could tell the full, dreadful story, in all its glory, to the receptionist. I might get time to think while they were twittering at the reception.

I don't know if I fell asleep or if the doctors gave me a sedative. I woke up, and the room was quiet. Soft lights were on, but no one was in the room apart from me. I could hear the beeping of the equipment. My head had a dull ache, but it wasn't painful.

Everything came flooding back to me, so there was no memory loss to save me from the anxiety of the events. There was a clock on the wall. It was dark outside, so I took it as 9 pm, not 9 am.

It was peaceful. If I could lie here until the disaster zone I created, sorted itself out, I could re-enter the world.

As Keith and Sandra entered the room, my fairy godmother was obviously in bed and unable to grant me my wish. Why those two? Why not the handsome Mike to sweep me up and take me away from all this?

"Oh, she's awake," said Sandra to Keith. As if he couldn't see for himself, my eyes were open.

"So, she is!" he answered.

It was like watching the muppet show!

They had serious faces on again. However, this was a more serious look, not so much the usual disapproving one.

"Tell me," I demanded, "what has happened now?"

"We've got a lot to tell you, maybe, you're not quite ready to hear it all," said Keith.

Sandra nodded with the gravest of faces.

"Oh, for fuck's sake, Keith, spit it out. I need to know everything, NOW," I shouted.

"Just with the head injury, it might be stressful," he continued.

"I swear the stress comes from not knowing, Keith, TELL ME WHAT IS HAPPENING!"

Keith and Sandra looked at each other, and Sandra nodded to him as if allowing him to tell me. Honestly, they were potty.

"First, the boys are fine. I've sent them to the hotel. They will change and eat dinner, and then they will come to see you. By the way, did you've to stay at the most expensive hotel in the area?"

Right, this was a good start. Seeing the boys would be so good right now.

"I'm glad the boys are okay. I'll pay any hotel bills," I replied.

Keith and Sandra nodded simultaneously as if they approved of this. They informed me they were staying at the hotel too. Yes, I would pay for them too!

"So, next up, your friend Mike and the boat's skipper have been arrested."

The news stung me; my head started spinning. Mike was with me the whole time. I could tell the police this.

Keith must have seen my summing up of the situation.

"There are no charges at this stage; it's a precautionary measure. The investigators found blood marks on the boat, which they will analyse. You will get to speak to Ispettore Colombo in the morning to give your version of what happened. Antonio is still missing."

I couldn't take it all in—blood marks on the boat. When Antonio was on the boat with us, there was no violence. Mike threw his phone out onto the Lake, but that was all. Did the skipper do something to Antonio? He seemed a nice guy, not someone who would hurt anyone. There was no need for anyone to harm Antonio. I couldn't believe Mike would've instructed the skipper to hurt him either.

The scenario felt like a beautiful crystal vase smashing into a thousand pieces. Then all the little slivers of glass cut into you. I was lying there, doubting my judgement and my memory. Had I misjudged the situation? Had I put my trust in someone just because they were famous? Had I acted like a teenager and thrown all regard for my safety out the window?

It had been so easy to fall into the fairytale. I felt like I was floating in a dream. Now I had crash-landed back to earth. I wanted to scream. My head hurt; I felt like my heart was beating out of my chest. Then I started to cry uncontrollably. This was uncharacteristic of me. I heard Sandra instruct Keith to get a nurse.

Chapter 22

They must have sedated me; when I woke up, the sun was streaming through the hospital window. At least the headache had subsided.

My boys were sitting at my bedside, slumped on two chairs, fast asleep. This made me smile briefly. I was glad they were sleeping and not crying over my bed all night. Under the circumstances and the shock, it would've been understandable.

I looked around—another positive—there was no sign of Sandra or Keith. My head was clearer. I lay there in the silence, able to think. After outpouring with emotion, I realised I didn't hear what had happened with Tim and his wife.

I felt sorry for her now. The lengths Tim had gone to when he couldn't contact me were disturbing. I wondered how it had all unfolded for Jess to end up here with her daughter.

Then my thoughts turned to Mike. I was sure he hadn't done anything. I had known him briefly, but what I had experienced was a considerate and kind guy, not a murderer. I had to be able to tell Ispettore Colombo all this and sort it out this morning.

The boys stirred.

"Morning, mum," said Dan, yawning. How is your head? The doctor said you will be fine, with no cracks in the skull or anything!"

This was good news. I hadn't considered whether Tim's wife had seriously injured me. So, when Dan told me there was no permanent damage, I was glad I hadn't added this to my list of things to worry about.

"Oh, that is at least something, Dan," I sighed. "What happened at the police station?"

"Well, we were interviewed separately," said Dan," we just told the guy everything we knew from when Tim came to the door. Then they told us to go to the hotel but not to head back to the UK until they said so."

"Well, I suppose that makes sense."

Dan continued awkwardly, "When we got to the hotel, the woman was there, his wife?"

My heart sank.

"Anyway, we were unsure what to do but decided to speak to her."

"Oh, what did she say?" I asked, not sure if I wanted to hear. My boys were caring; they probably got that from Keith, which I hated to admit.

"Well, she wanted to get it off her chest, how you had stolen her man!"

"That's fair," I replied weakly.

"Then, just at that, Tim arrived back. He told her to be quiet and leave us alone. Under the circumstances, I felt that was rich coming from him!"

I found this incredible. Tim's wife had caught him cheating, but he was telling his wife to be quiet.

"That is rich coming from him," I agreed. "I want to speak to her and apologise for everything, I know it might not help, but I've messed up here!"

"Well, that isn't all," Dan continued. "She tried to argue back, but he grabbed her arm and told her to control herself. It looked more like he was controlling her. I asked her if she was okay, and she nodded. Then this older woman appeared with luggage and the little girl."

"Who was she?" I asked.

"Tim's mother, it seems, had flown over with his wife. However, Tim instructed her to take the daughter back home for school. So, a taxi arrived and off they went to the airport. I could tell his wife wanted to go with them, but Tim reminded her she had to stay in case you were going to press charges against her for assault. He also said they needed to sort things out! However, the way he behaved, sorting things out, looked like he wouldn't allow her to complain about his actions!"

I was quiet. I'd been complicit in an affair, thinking it was all fun and games. Tim hadn't shown any signs of this behaviour before, well, at least I hadn't noticed. However, when I decided to come to Italy alone on Friday, definite red flags were starting to show that had ended up in this mess.

"I'm not going to press any charges. Do you think his wife is okay?" I asked, "Have you seen her since?"

"Well, we came over here not long after that and have not returned to the hotel yet. Dad and Sandra should be there just now."

I had a bad feeling, but wasn't sure if it was just because of everything that had happened.

"And no word on Antonio yet?" I enquired.

"No, your man Mike and the boat's skipper were arrested but dad said he told you this last night."

"Yes, he did!" I confirmed sadly. "Boys, I know I've only known Mike and the Skipper briefly, but I don't believe they are violent men."

The boys both nodded.

Dan said, "Yes, Mum, Mike approached Jack and me before we were split up for questioning. He was more concerned about whether we were okay and how you were, rather than himself. So, we agree; he seems like a decent guy."

My heart melted at this. Mike was concerned for my boys over his drama unfolding.

"Dan, can you contact the police and ask if Ispettore Colombo can come to the hospital to speak to me, or ask at the desk if they can discharge me? I can't lie here doing nothing!"

"Ok, mum, I'll see if I can grab us some breakfast too!"

Jack then woke up. He looked around dazed, then I could see him recalling the events.

"Mum, I feel as if we're in a crazy movie. What the hell!"

"I know, I wish the crazy movie wasn't quite as disturbing!" I replied.

Dan came back with coffee, crusty rolls, butter, and jam. Although I had an uneasy feeling dwelling in my core, I was hungry and gladly ate the food. I realised I hadn't eaten since the idyllic picnic less than 24 hours ago, when Mike wrapped me in his arms. We had sat there, naked under a tree with a blanket around us, sharing cheese and grapes. How could it go from that to this?

The doctor told me I was free to go, but to take it easy. I smiled ruefully; I didn't know what would be easy about the day ahead.

I showered. I'd been moaning incessantly about Sandra and Keith; however, credit where credit is due. Sandra had the good sense to give the boys fresh clothes for me to bring to the hospital. There was also a bag of toiletries and my makeup bag. This was kind of her, and she could have ignored what I might have needed due to how I treated her. Thankfully, I was able to make myself look almost normal.

By the time I was ready, Dan had managed to speak to Ispettore Colombo, who told him we could go straight to the police station. He was sending a car for us.

As we went to the hospital exit, Jack exclaimed,

"Oh, we forgot to warn you about this, mum!"

There were photographers and reporters everywhere. They were like a cackle of hyenas. With all the drama, I kept forgetting that Mike was famous. A Hollywood actor. This wasn't something the press would hold to the confines of Bellagio. The whole bloody world would know about it. I hadn't even considered the reverb from this.

Luckily, the police car awaited us as Ispettore Colombo had promised. The police officer in the passenger seat jumped out, helping us escape from the hyenas and into the vehicle. I told Dan and Jack they should go to the hotel and relax by the pool. They had done a night shift, and I would meet them there once I had spoken to Ispettore Colombo.

Jack and Dan protested, but there wasn't anything they could do. There was no point in them hanging about the police station while the police interviewed me.

The kind police officer driving agreed to drop them off first. There were more paparazzi outside the hotel. I was glad to stay in the haven of the car. The hotel security staff must have recognised my boys and helped them inside the hotel. I was pleased they weren't letting anyone in who wasn't a guest. There was a security man stationed at the door.

The police parked outside the station door. More photographers were flashing their cameras and shouting.

The police officer protectively put his arm around me and guided me inside.

I was glad of the police station's sanctity. Outside, bedlam was everywhere I looked. And here I was, the creator of this disaster. I made a personal note to myself to consider my actions in the future.

Ispettore Colombo greeted me at the reception window.

His spoken English was excellent, and I was grateful we could easily communicate. I could have attempted to speak Italian, but I wouldn't have been able to explain what had happened fully.

He ushered me into an interview room, and a police officer was with him. She fetched me water, and then we were ready to start. Both of them sat opposite me.

Ispettore Colombo asked me to tell him my version of events from the very beginning, right back to my arrival in Italy and why I was travelling alone.

He already knew I'd been having an affair with Tim. He had seen, first hand, Tim's wife shoving me over. He had asked if I wanted to press charges for this. Which, of course, I didn't. He nodded in agreement, and this was probably the correct answer. Once he established this, he made a quick call, I believe it was to Jess, as he told whoever he was talking to they were free to go home.

I started talking about meeting Mike. As I retold the tale, I couldn't believe it was me talking about how I had spent my last two days—my flight here and the taxi journey, the dreamy Saturday afternoon that seemed in the distant past now.

Ispettore Colombo and the police officer listened intently without interrupting. Then I started to tell them where I first met Antonio in the hotel bar. I told them this was before Mike collected me for dinner.

Ispettore Colombo was highly interested to learn that Antonio never told me he was Tim's associate in Italy.

He reaffirmed, "So, Antonio never told you he knew Tim or knew who you were?"

"That is correct," I replied, "at no point did he say who he was. I only found this out when we discovered him taking pictures on the boat."

I then proceeded to talk about the dinner. A few times, Ispettore Colombo confirmed that Mike hadn't left my sight apart from a brief visit to the restaurant's toilet.

I explained the boat trip across to Mike's villa, Antonio's surprise appearance on the boat, and how Antonio told us he knew Tim, who had asked him to spy on me.

Ispettore Colombo and the police officer listened intently. I knew this was the key part of the investigation.

I explained the exact chain of events as much as I could. At no point was Antonio injured or threatened with his life. There had been no violence. Mike launched Antonio's phone into the lake and cautioned him not to call Tim when he returned to the shore. Mike grabbed the lapels of Antonio's jacket; however, he didn't shake him violently or punch him. I confirmed I was sure no harm had come to Antonio when I was there.

Ispettore Colombo wanted to know where the skipper fit in. Again, I could only tell him what I learned. As far as I was concerned, when Mike and I disembarked, the skipper took Antonio back to Bellagio. There was no real reason why the skipper would've harmed him, either. He even had the money Mike had given him to let Antonio buy a new phone.

The next part of the event was embarrassing to talk through, as Mike and I had obviously been in a compromising situation. I knew I had to tell them everything, as there could have been CCTV. A member of Mike's staff could have seen Mike and me in the pool in the height of passion.

I could see Ispettore Colombo and the police officer trying not to smirk at my recollections; however, it got serious again when Ispettore Colombo questioned if Mike had been out of my sight. He wanted to know a lot about what time things happened.

I explained to Ispettore Colombo that I hadn't taken my watch that night. I had put my phone on silent and disregarded it for several hours due to Tim's incessant calls.

I explained that Mike and I fell asleep on the sofa beside the bar. I thought it was around 3 am, but we woke up just after sunrise.

"So, while you were sleeping, Mike Maloney could have left you and returned without your knowledge?" Ispettore Colombo asked.

I didn't like this question.

"Well, he could have, but I'm sure I would've sensed it if he had left and returned later."

We were stuck together like glue!

Ispettore Colombo smiled at me.

"Iona, you told me you had wine in the afternoon, then again in the evening, and drank whiskey. Then you had a very energetic activity. (He coughed after he said this, and I cringed.)

Is it possible you fell into a profound sleep, and Mike may have left without you noticing and returned later?"

I didn't want to believe this could be true, and I was sure Mike wouldn't leave my side. Yet Ispettore Colombo presented me with a reasonable scenario within the timescale.

"When you put it like that, Ispettore, I can't rule it out. All I can say is I honestly don't think Mike left my side, but I can't account for those hours."

I felt heavy-hearted. I didn't think Mike had done anything to Antonio. However, I had let him down, since I could only give him an alibi for the waking hours. I felt we woke up the same way we went to sleep. Entwined in each other, merged. Due to the position, we woke up, I was sure Mike hadn't moved from my side.

I suddenly longed to see him.

"Can I speak to Mike, please?" I asked Ispettore Colombo.

"Not at the moment," Ispettore Colombo said, "this is a missing person investigation. I'm waiting on blood samples to come back from the lab. These results will depend on whether I can release Mr Maloney and Skipper Capaldi.

Can I write him a note, then, please?

"You can, but I must read it before giving it to him."

I nodded, and the police officer gave me paper and a pen.

"Dear Mike

I can't believe our amazing time has turned into this bedlam. I know in my heart you didn't do anything. I'm sorry about my life drama involving you. I'm out here hoping to find answers soon and get you out.

Love Iona x"

Ispettore Colombo read the note and nodded that he would give it to Mike.

"For now, please return to your hotel and stay in Italy!"

I nodded, and the police officer escorted me to a waiting car. There was more flash photography and people shouting questions at me. Talking with the police had taken a couple of hours, and I was exhausted and hungry.

Chapter 22

I was now back in business with my phone. The boys charged it for me and returned it to me at the hospital. I called ahead to say I was coming to the hotel. They told me the manager said to use the kitchen entrance. I told the police officer who was driving me back to the hotel.

On the journey back, I looked through my phone. There were missed calls from the day before from Tim, then from the boys, and Keith. Once Tim had alerted them to my supposed kidnapping, they had all frantically been calling me. Tim creating this level of fuss over me was unbelievable.

The boys were waiting for me at the hotel kitchen entrance. We quickly went to the lobby and into the bar, where Keith and Sandra sat on sofas.

I sat down. They ordered sandwiches and coffee. A delicious selection of sandwiches arrived perfectly cut and arranged on a beautiful platter. Usually, I would have photographed the platter, but I was too weary for this. The coffee was in a gorgeous coffee pot with matching cups and saucers. The exquisiteness wasn't lost on me, but the desire to record it all was too much effort.

We ate and drank. Everyone was exhausted. The last 24 hours were far from normal.

Keith spoke first, "Is there any update from the police?"

"No," I replied. Ispettore Colombo wanted my statement about everything. He says I can't provide an alibi for Mike for the hours I was asleep. He is right, but I know Mike had nothing to do with this."

Keith said, "I agree with you, I don't think he did. I spoke to him, and he seems decent."

Keith agreed with me; this was new!

"However, your man Tim, with whom you've been having an affair. His actions are bizarre! He was mad at his wife for pushing you, yet he's the one who is cheating!"

I had to agree that Tim's actions were getting worse and worse. I hadn't spoken to Tim or given him my thoughts on what had happened. When I say thoughts, I mean I would give him a rollicking.

"I agree with you, Keith!" I replied. "There must be something in the air, the two of us agreeing on two consecutive things!"

Then we all laughed, even Sandra. It was good to have a couple of moments of humour in this mess.

"The boys said Tim and his wife are still here. I need to apologise to her, then speak with him. I'm not looking forward to it, but I need to. He arranged for Antonio, the guy who is now missing, to follow me!"

Dan spoke, "Oh, there's an update on that, Mum! He said Inspector Colombo called and said she could go home, as you weren't pressing charges. So, he more or less said she immediately headed to the airport. I saw Tim an hour ago, and he said it was just him here now."

"Oh, really," I replied. You would think Tim would've kept her here and tried to save his marriage! Or maybe she wanted to get back to her daughter."

"Maybe she doesn't want to save her marriage," Sandra piped in. "I know I wouldn't want to if that happened to me!"

I couldn't argue with that. I decided to go to my room to lie down, and then I would find Tim and talk to him about everything. If only Antonio would turn up to end the nightmare.

I arranged with them all to meet at about 5.30 pm for dinner at 6 pm.

It was only noon, and I took the lift to my room. I managed to navigate the lobby area without bumping into anyone, which I was glad about. I went into my room, set an alarm for 1.30 pm, kicked off my shoes, and fell back on the bed. The amazing bed welcomed me onboard. I sank into it and fell asleep instantly.

I heard the alarm going off and felt disoriented. I couldn't think where I was. The darkened room had daylight streaming through a crack in the curtains. Then I remembered. I was in the middle of Bedlam in Bellagio!

I turned around and got the fright of my life. Tim was lying beside me on the bed.

What the fuck?

I stared at Tim. He had a strange look about him. He no longer looked like the guy I used to know. Not that I knew him that well at all, as it turned out!

"Tim," I started, "what the hell were you playing at getting Antonio to spy on me?"

"Shhh," he said, "I shouldn't have done that, but can we talk about this later? I need your help!"

"My help?" I repeated, not sure where this was going. He was deviating from the facts I wanted to discuss with him.

"Yes, please listen. I think Antonio has just gone off the radar. He was involved with dodgy stuff. I know where he might be. Will you come with me to check?"

Seriously!

"Why haven't you told the police this, Tim? Mike and the skipper are facing a murder charge. They are in police cells and

232

have no idea what is happening. For fuck's sake!"

"I know, I know, but please hear me out! I don't know if I'm right. I know he uses derelict buildings near here and may be hiding out. If I'm wrong and he isn't there, I will have led the police on a wild goose chase. I want to check it out first. I promise we can alert the police if we find him! I'll drive, and you can take pictures if we see him. I don't want him to see us. Then we can show the police and sort all this mess out."

The thought of sorting this quickly appealed to me. It would be worth it if this got Mike out of jail.

"How far away are we talking about, Tim?"

"About half an hour's drive from here! I've a car I picked up at the airport! Let's keep it to ourselves until we're sure. It will just upset everyone more."

I decided to go along with this. I thought the more people involved might jeopardise finding Antonio quickly! Tim and I could chat in the car on the way there. I told him to bring it to the side entrance, and I would meet him there. The others were at the pool, and I would be back long before we had arranged to meet for dinner. If I mentioned it to Keith and Sandra, they would spend an hour talking me out of going.

Tim picked me up at the side entrance. He was wearing sunglasses and looked very happy for a man whose wife had found out he was cheating on her.

"You look great!" he said as he drove us out of Bellagio.

What?

"Thanks, Tim, but I don't think this is a time for compliments! Let's chat about your wife finding out about us. How is she? I feel terrible for her and my part in it."

"Iona, she knocked you over, she could've killed you!"

"Tim, she had come face to face with the woman having an affair with her husband, it's understandable. In all honesty, I would've done the same in the circumstances. How the hell did she find out anyway?"

"Well, you were missing, and I was so worried. I was pacing about, and I left my phone lying unlocked. She read the messages and worked it out pretty quickly. I told her I was coming here to save you. Once I knew your boys hadn't heard from you, I was getting plane tickets organised. She begged me not to come, but I had to. The next thing I know, she's in Bellagio with my mother and daughter. I was mad with her!"

"You were mad with her? That's a bit rich, Tim! Can you imagine how she must've felt?"

"It doesn't matter how she felt, and she was interfering."

Interfering? With what?

"Tim, she's your wife. She isn't interfering; she has every right to be mad!"

"Whose side are you on?" Tim shouted.

His face was red, his veins pulsing on his forehead. His eyes were dark with rage.

"Hers!" I shouted back. "Why didn't you travel home with her and look after her? You could've shown compassion rather than letting her travel home alone!"

"I didn't let her travel alone; she went home with my mother and daughter!"

Liar! Although I knew this already, he was having an affair with me after all!

Based on what the boys had told me, I knew this wasn't true.

"|What the fuck are you telling lies for, Tim? My son saw your daughter leave last night. He said you told him your wife headed home this morning after I confirmed I wasn't pressing charges! She couldn't leave the country last night when your mother and daughter left!"

"Don't fucking question me, Iona," Tim yelled turning to me shaking with anger.

"Tim, keep your eye on the…."

Chapter 23

It was a near miss. A truck coming along the narrow road swerved to avoid us. Tim had careered into the middle of the road in all his rage.

As I had shouted to warn him, he managed to pull hard on the steering wheel to the right, but it was a small hire car, so it started to spin out of control.

I was screaming, and Tim was yelling. The truck missed us by centimetres, and we stopped on the grassy verge, narrowly missing a signpost on the road.

Smoke was everywhere from the burning rubber. The truck had stopped. Recovering from the shock, I couldn't speak. In the wing mirror, I saw the driver getting out of the truck, and he looked mad.

Tim was silent. I turned to look at him to check for injuries. He was sweating, but there was no sign of any trauma. He was looking in his rear-view mirror. The car engine was still running. We had stopped facing the same direction we had been travelling in. Before I could say a word, he put the car in gear and frantically sped us off down the road. I could see the truck driver shaking his fist.

I was shocked to the core. I sat still, not knowing what to think about Tim's lies and rage.

"Do you see what you made me do, Iona!" Tim said, "We nearly got killed, and then everything would be wasted."

"What I made you do, Tim!" I cried, my voice shaking. "What do you mean, everything will be wasted?"

I admit I was getting scared.

He was looking and acting like a madman, not the good-looking Tim I shagged every Wednesday afternoon. Not the guy I thought had the same understanding of our affair as I did.

He must have realised he was acting crazy.

"Right, okay, don't worry," he said more gently. "Once you see what I mean, you'll realise it's all fine."

At this point, I decided keeping him calm was the best idea, for fear of any more near-death road crashes. I could call out this bizarre behaviour once Tim parked the car and wasn't in charge of the wheel.

For now, I nodded my head and tried a smile.

Tim smiled back and put his hand on my knee. "There," he said, "this is better. The two of us driving along the Italian road, not a care in the world."

'Not a care in the world,' we're in a fucking disaster movie!

It is incredible how quickly your feelings can change. The touch of his hand on my knee made my skin crawl. Yet, three days ago, I was supposed to be arriving here with Tim for a "dirty weekend." Here I was, wondering if I ever really even knew him. Was I so unattached to our affair that I never saw his flawed personality? Did it not matter to me what he was like, as it was only one afternoon a week?"

I smiled again, as sweetly as I could. There was something far wrong here. My gut, instinct, and intuition were on fire. I needed to act this out until I could get out of the car. I didn't feel safe. I shouldn't have agreed to come with Tim to look for Antonio. The thought of helping Mike had overpowered me. And worse still, I realised I had left my phone sitting by my bedside table in my hotel room. What a stupid mistake for me to make. I had no way of contacting anyone.

I had to help myself. I leaned my head to the side and looked at Tim,

"Yes, this is lovely," I managed to say convincingly.

I did think I was a good actor, so I had better make sure I was. I put my hand on top of Tim's hand. He smiled, pleased I hadn't kept the argument going. My heart was pounding in my chest. What had happened to my life in this brief time?

We drove along, my hand on his. The further we got from Bellagio, the more disturbed I felt.

At last, Tim put the indicator on and turned right up a single-track road. I noticed he hadn't hesitated at the turning. He wasn't using Sat Nav either. It seemed he had been here before. I resigned myself to the fact that he knew where he was going. He'd tricked me into coming here!

We went up the road a little, and buildings came into my view. They looked like outhouses, stables, or something, not actual houses. Getting nearer, I could see boarded-up windows and derelict buildings.

This didn't fill me with confidence. I wasn't sure how I managed to keep my cool, but I had the most remarkable instinct to stay alert. If I had allowed myself to feel fear, I might have lost control. I could do this. I had to.

"So, is this where you think Antonio is?" I asked as casually as I could.

"Oh, he's here all right," Tim said, smiling and looking incredibly happy considering the turmoil.

My stomach churned. He had told me we were coming to see if Antonio was hiding here, and now, suddenly, he was here. There was another car parked further up towards one of the buildings.

He parked the car on the wasteland. I didn't want to make any rash moves. He pulled his hand away to open the car door. So, I motioned to open mine, and he didn't flinch. Gladly, I go out, taking deep breaths to calm my nervous system. Yes, I had learned this on another of those courses my employer sent me on; however, on that course, I just breathed. I didn't start an affair with another of the delegates!

I wanted to run. I'd never experienced such an urge to run away. (Well, apart from a time in France many years before, that's another story for another day!) I kept my cool using every fibre of my being. There was a fucking mystery to solve here.

Tim came round to my side of the car and took my hand.

Bloody moron!

"This way," he said, smiling from ear to ear.

This was a guy who had nearly killed us in a car crash fifteen minutes ago, and was now acting like we had simply been on a roller coaster.

We went round to the front of one of the buildings. There was an open door that looked like an unused office entrance. It had an open sign on it which I found strange as we were in the arsehole of nowhere and not a person in sight.

Tim pushed the door open and went through first. This was probably an excellent time to run, but I needed answers to the Antonio mystery. I wish my curiosity hadn't improved, but I had Mr Drop Dead Gorgeous to break out of jail.

Chapter 24

"We're here!" Tim called out, which made me shiver.

So, Antonio was here and was expecting us! The plot thickened! What the hell was I dealing with?

"In here," replied a familiar voice with an Italian accent.

Tim pushed open a door. Beyond was a comfortably furnished open-plan room. It had flooring, a leather sofa, and two leather chairs. A dining table and chairs sat behind the sofa, and there was a kitchen area with a large fridge.

Antonio was sitting slouched on a chair, larger than life, with no marks on him. He hadn't suffered any violence.

He was wearing the same clothes from Saturday night. Sweat dripped from his brow, so I decided to keep a distance as I was sure there would be an unpleasant odour from him.

He looked at me and smirked. His persona from when we met had changed. He was a good actor; I'll give him that. The 'poor me, I was just doing my work colleague a favour' routine from Saturday night on the boat might as well be someone else, and the charmer I met in the hotel bar. This Antonio was verging on arrogant and confident! A game was being played here, and I had to figure out what it was.

I was so bloody confused. However, the relief that Antonio was alive, and Mike wasn't guilty of murder was palpable. I gained strength from this knowledge; my aim of setting Mike free from jail seemed closer. I would celebrate this fact if the current situation weren't so dire.

The reality was that none of this was normal. What the hell was going on?

I picked my words carefully. I didn't know where my ability to remain calm came from. I hoped for a reasonable explanation for what had become Bedlam in Bellagio. However, I wasn't confident that there would be any reason applied here.

"Antonio, I'm so glad you're alive," I stated with conviction; I was glad he was alive, as all accusations of murder vanished in an instant. "We thought something awful had happened to you. The police suggested murder as a possibility, but here you are!

Antonio shrugged and smirked. I wanted to slap his face, but I used my 'Nerves of Steel.'

"And Tim, you knew Antonio was here all along?" I questioned.

Tim looked at me as if he were an injured animal. I decided to say nothing else until they told me more. I needed to play along with this for now.

Tim put his arm around me, and my skin crawled. "Have a seat, Iona, then I can explain everything."

My legs felt weak, and I knew this wasn't over. Keep playing along, I told myself. I had to use all my reserves and intelligence. I sat down, and Tim offered me a bottle of water. I was thirsty but now wary of everything. When I realised the cap was intact, I was delighted. At least I knew I could drink it without worrying they had laced it with drugs.

I used to think I watched too many dramas on TV, but now that I was in a precarious position, I might as well use any insight that kept me alert.

I drank the icy water gratefully.

"That has certainly quenched my thirst," I said. "Tim's wife knocked me out yesterday, Antonio, so I think the painkillers the hospital gave me are making me thirsty.

Tim's ex-wife turned up and she has a good punch!"

I knew I was talking shite, but when everything is chaotic, talking shite might be the best policy.

Antonio shrugged again and glared at me. For the first time, I thought he could be dangerous. I hadn't considered him other than the oaf who followed me about on Tim's instructions, but now I saw something menacing!

Tim looked at me like a love-struck teenager. It was off-putting and creepy. However, I smiled.

" Okay, what is happening here then?" I asked like a concerned friend. "Spill the beans."

I could see that Tim was happy to see my inquisitiveness. I made a mental note to continue acting this way.

"Well, babe, do you remember who suggested this trip?" he asked.

"Yes," I replied, "you suggested it. I said it was fine for me, but I asked if it wouldn't be difficult for you to get away. You told me you could say it was a work trip."

"Good," said Tim, as if I had passed a school spelling test. "So, once you agreed, I knew I could progress with a plan I've had for a while."

A Plan?

This revelation unhinged me, but I decided to engage him,

"Oh, what plan is this?" I asked calmly.

"Since we met, I can't stop thinking about you. I daydream about you when I'm at work. I long to be with you, and Wednesday can't come fast enough. I wake up thinking about you every morning. It feels like a travesty that we're not together permanently."

Shit!

I didn't like the sound of this. I couldn't force myself to say I thought of him all the time. I didn't. He wanted to hear this. I managed to smile at him and nod my head. I'm unsure if it looked convincing, but I tried my best. I hoped he didn't pick up that no words came from my mouth.

Luckily, he continued talking.

"I reckoned you felt the same, but I knew you didn't want to be the one to break up a family.

Fucking hell, he had no idea how wrong he was. I never wanted to be with him on a full-time basis. There were no gut-wrenching feelings of love coming from me!

I could feel my heart beating faster, and I didn't know what was coming next.

You need to keep it together, I told myself. I smiled again.

"So, this is when I started thinking how I could make it easier for us to be together. I thought, once we were here, I could get us away to a new life together."

What the fuck was he on about?

Now, I had due cause to be worried.

He seemed in a zone as he laid out the plan like a man who had been hypnotised, so I let him continue. I was speechless anyway!

"So, I managed to source Antonio. I'm sorry, but I said he's a colleague of mine because he isn't. He has contacts to help people disappear to start a new life."

I felt the blood drain from my face. I wanted to stand up and start running fast, as far as I could get away from here, away from Tim, and away from this mad situation. However, at this point, I couldn't work out how to escape. I felt like a trapped animal.

"A new life," I managed to say.

Tim was on a roll now,

"Yes, Antonio has a contact in Switzerland. He can arrange new passports and a new identity.

I can't believe you nearly messed it up, Iona, coming here yourself, but I knew I had Antonio on the ground to watch you. I can forgive you for the Mike situation, as you're here now, where I can keep an eye on you. Antonio and his wife want to disappear, too.

When the incident happened on the boat, he thought it was a suitable time to start a chain of events. He managed to cut himself and rub some blood inside the boat, which raised suspicion about Mike. Then he got his wife to say he was missing.

Another contact said they saw him getting onto the boat, but confirmed to the police he didn't return. So, we knew we could raise an alarm about your safety and get Mike out of the way!"

Now I knew I was in danger. Tim was a stalker who wanted to kidnap me and change my identity. I sat there, frozen, trying to work out what to do. I was scared and alone with these two nutjobs. I didn't know whether to laugh or cry at Tim's plan. I had no idea what expression my face showed. I tried not to look terrified.

I was thinking anyone normal would tell someone they liked them. Then there would be discussions about whether there were enough feelings to make a life together, as well as considering the rest of the people it would affect. Why did we have to run away to be together? I wondered if he realised I wouldn't have wanted a relationship, so he decided this was the way forward. To kidnap me and control my life?

"I know it's a huge surprise," said Tim. "Think about it, though. You've all your money, and you can use it for us to set up again. You said you had around £750,000 accumulated. So, we can pay Antonio his £100,000 fee and have plenty left over!"

Oh my god, what an arsehole!

Why had I bragged about my excellent investment skills to Tim? I would happily have kicked myself up the arse for such stupidity! This fucking moron wanted to steal me away to a new life and use my fucking money to do it. I was beyond angry. I wanted to explode. I sat there boiling inside, fused, ready to detonate.

Internally, I was talking myself down to stay calm. A huge life lesson learned: don't brag about the wealth you are accumulating to anyone. What an idiot I'd been going on about how I managed to do it.

I had to wonder if it was just my money he was after.

I started speaking. I wasn't sure where the words came from as I was in a whirlwind of terror and livid. I couldn't mention my money. I wouldn't have been able to talk about it without losing my temper with him.

"So why did you involve my boys? Why did you bring them here, and let your wife and daughter find out?"

Tim began to rant, "Well, we had to make it seem real. I wanted to make sure everyone thought Mike kidnapped you, and that Antonio had come to harm. Otherwise, you would still be acting out of character with Mike. I needed to make sure I could split you up from him to talk sense into you as you wouldn't answer your fucking phone. I'm trying not to be furious about you and him. I couldn't believe it when you said you were coming out here yourself. I thought we would just rebook the trip and execute the plan then. But oh no, you had to come here then cheat on me and nearly waste everything, but don't worry, it's all back on track."

I wasn't worried I was fucking traumatised! Tim was using Mike as part of his plan to steal me away to a new identity!

"Once we have our new identity, I know I'll be able to make sure you won't act like this again."

My blood ran cold, I was in the presence of a madman who was going to keep me in a cage and control me.

"My wife found out sooner than she should have, her fault for looking at my phone and meddling! So, just her to sort out, now," he said calmly.

I was alert, he told me his wife had gone home.

I needed to keep him onside. Was his wife in danger? If she was, it was my bloody fault.

Shit, shit, shit.

How was I going to sort this? I needed to stay alive, keep my current identity, save his wife, return to my boys, and free Mike. This was a lot to take in with a head injury. My fairy tale had become a bloody nightmare. Now I had to become a CIA-style agent and take my life in my hands on a Monday afternoon in the Italian sun when I could have been having a late lunch with wine, looking at Mike's gorgeous face.

I choose my words carefully,

"I'm sorry for what I've done, Tim, and I shouldn't have upset you and worried you. Where is Jess?"

Tim smiled, "She's in there," he said, pointing to a door.

Fucking hell, my mind raced; was she injured? Was she alive?

"Is she okay?" I managed to ask.

"Yes," said Tim, "she's fine for now."

I felt sick.

For now?

What were his intentions for her?

I had to pretend I was happy with his plan. There was no other way. I had to get his trust to get access to Jess. I decided to divert the conversation about his wife to Tim's plan for our new life. The less he thought about his wife and the more he thought about us, the less likely he would go into the room and cause her harm in the interim.

"So, what do we need to organise for this plan to go smoothly?" I asked, all matter of fact. "You should simply have told me, Tim, it's exciting. I can't believe you organised all this for us. I'm so sad I came without you and did what I did."

"Hey," he smiled, "come here, I'm so happy you love the plan."

Then he took me in his arms and kissed me. It was horrid. You can go off someone's kiss quickly when they divulge a scary personality. This time last week, I enjoyed kissing Tim. I was thinking of our weekend in Italy. I wanted his company. Now it was like kissing a maniac, and though he never had bad breath, it felt like he had.

I had to respond to his kiss and ensure I saved Jess and me. It was like looking at a crazy situation unfolding through a window. I tried to see what was available around the room, which I could use to defend myself or go on the attack.

I remembered reading an article by an ex-SAS operative who said you need to see what objects you could use if you're threatened. Lamps, forks, glasses, knives, and tables are all weapons when launched at someone with force.

I attended self-defence classes about eight years ago, so I knew moves that might help me. I was against two men and knew I would need more than strength. I was physically fit, but so was Tim. Antonio didn't look particularly fit, but I was sure he was strong.

I was thinking all this while Tim kissed me. It distracted me from the kiss. I was so relieved when he stopped for air, the fucking psycho.

"Right," he said, "We must gather our stuff before people know you're missing."

In all the shock of what was unfolding, I forgot my family would start to miss me once I hadn't appeared for dinner as arranged. They would go to the room to look for me, but I wouldn't. This gave me a little hope.

"Okay," I said cheerily. We have time. I told my family I would sleep until seven and prepare to meet for dinner at 8 pm I told them not to disturb me before that."

This was a lie, as I had arranged 6 pm for dinner, but I wanted to give Tim a false sense of security about how much time he had before my family discovered I was missing.

"Ah, that's terrific," Tim exclaimed, as if I'd told him he'd won the lottery. "It's only 3.30 pm; we've loads of time."

So, it was at least two hours until my family would discover I was missing, but Tim thought it was longer.

"We need to get our belongings from the hotel," Tim said. "Antonio needs to fetch his wife, too!"

Antonio hadn't said a lot apart from nodding in agreement.

I reckoned Tim was excited that I agreed with his plan. I hedged my bets and decided to suggest a way forward.

"So, let's think this through logically," I said, as if I were planning a bus trip.

"It is about 45 minutes back to the hotel. Then it will take you some time to gather all our belongings. Then it will be a 45-minute return journey. I should stay here. If my boys or ex-husband see me going in or out of the hotel, they will ask many questions, as I'm supposed to be resting."

Tim nodded in agreement. I now had him onside, and I didn't want to waste my chance. He hadn't mentioned his wife again, and I decided I wouldn't either. I knew where she was, so if I could get them to trust me and go for our belongings, I would have my chance.

Then Tim said,

"Although, do we need any belongings. We're starting a new life."

Fuck!

Then I remembered he wanted all my money. This would help.

"Well, Tim, I've got my laptop at the hotel. I can get into it and access all my investments. Then I can work out how to transfer them, and we can start our new life with all the money. But I need to do it before anyone reports me as a missing person. Once I disappear, they could trace me if I access them. This way, when anyone realises I've transferred the funds elsewhere, we'll be long gone!"

Please agree on this!

I didn't know what I would do if Tim managed to get back and I hadn't escaped. There was no bloody way he was getting his dirty hands on my cash! But I needed to convince him to leave me here.

"See, you're the smart one," Tim beamed.

"You're right, I never thought of this, and we want to have the funds with us as soon as possible."

"Exactly, Tim," I don't want us to be scrimping when we don't need to. No one will bat an eyelid if you're at the hotel, as you're supposed to be there. I would say leave my case in my room, as my boys would recognise it if they saw you with it. You can put my clothes in bags to avoid questions about why you've got my suitcase."

I knew this suggestion was foolish, as his raising suspicion would be great for me, but I wanted him to think I was totally on his side. I did think there was a possibility that if anybody saw Tim with a carrier bag full of clothes, they would think it odd anyway. I hoped he would look cagey or maniacal and cause my boys or Keith to raise an alarm.

"Yes, I'll do that," Tim agreed. "Antonio, can you be back here by 6.30 pm? Iona can transfer your funds, and then we can leave and be in Lucerne by 10 pm!"

"Ah, it has all worked out!" Antonio grinned.

I wanted to punch him in his big fat gut! Transfer his funds my arse, he would be getting nil!

"We will be here by 6.30 pm," he confirmed, "with my big car for the four of us."

Okay, the four of us meant the wife wasn't coming with us. The dread reached the pit of my stomach.

"We will just leave your wife here, and at some point, someone will find her," Antonio said to Tim.

Tim nodded in agreement and looked at me.

I nodded too.

Yes, you absolute pyscho fucker just leave your poor wife here to thirst to death in the heat. Don't care that she's the mother of your child.

My head was banging. This situation was treacherous; I needed to keep up the act.

"Yeah, just leave her in there," I said. "I don't even want to look at her; she could have killed me with that push yesterday. She's mental." I scowled.

Tim nodded, "I know, babe, I was so worried; she deserves to be left alone in the dark and scared."

"Please tell me the door is locked," I said, "she can't come out and have another go at me, can she?" I hoped I sounded pathetic and frightened.

"It is okay, Iona," Tim said, stroking my hair. "She's tied up and has duct tape over her mouth."

I wanted to be sick.

"Thank goodness," I cried out, at least they thought my angst was for me and not his poor wife.

"Is the door locked too?" I asked timidly.

"No, but she's tied to a pole in there, she isn't going anywhere, and we sedated her."

Absolute maniacs!

So, I had a sedated woman, tied up, that I had to set free within the next two hours. I wasn't sure of our location. There was daylight until about 9 pm. I needed another look outside at the surroundings while they were still here. I didn't want to waste time looking for an escape route while trying to wake Jess and get her up to speed on what was happening.

"Tim, can you come outside with me for air, please? Then I think I'll have a power nap on the sofa while you're away, so I'm fresh for our exit into Switzerland."

Tim smiled, pleased at my compliance.

What an arsehole.

.

"Come on then," he took my hand and led me outside. The spring sunshine had started to cool and felt nice on my face. Good, I thought, great weather for escaping. I considered we needed to get far enough away for safety, but we may need to be able to hide for a rest or until we could summon help.

Behind the buildings, there was a stream. I thought following the stream would be the best plan. Streams usually end up beside cottages or farms, where livestock may drink from. There were trees along the stream, which looked promising, too— somewhere to hide if necessary. I didn't want Tim to see me eyeing all this up, so I was looking around.

There are a lot of derelict buildings in this lovely countryside," I said. I'm surprised no one has snapped it up as a development."

Tim agreed, pleased I was acting like the Iona he knew. I pointed to a building opposite the stream, focusing all my attention on the building.

"These would be great for a game of hide and seek." I laughed.

Tim laughed, too. I wanted to plant the idea in his head that I would hide in these buildings. Then, when he returned, it would be the first place he would look for me when he realised I was missing. This could buy Jess and me more time to get further away.

When I was satisfied with the direction Jess and I were going, I yawned. I forced myself to cuddle Tim and hold him tightly. He held me as tightly back, and it felt like he might not let me go.

Tim led me back into the house with his arm around me. This was hard, bloody work.

I calculated I could usually walk about three miles an hour at normal walking speed. Tim's wife looked fit enough from what I could recall of our brief encounter. If I could get her onside quickly, I was sure we could get far enough from here before Tim and Antonio arrived back.

Tim found me a blanket,

"Here you're Iona, you lie down and rest."

Before this monster presented itself, there was a glimpse of the old Tim, the man I thought he was. I felt sorry for him for a split second, but it passed as quickly as that. It was amazing how your mind can fool you.

Now, it was time to go into survival mode. It could quickly turn nasty if Tim realised I was stringing him along. Look at the depths he had already gone to.

I cuddled up on the sofa with the blanket. "Ah, that feels good I said. I'll dream about Switzerland and the Alps until you get back. Please be as quick as you can!"

I was proud of my acting, although it was worrying how naturally I was fitting into the role.

"Tim leaned over and kissed my forehead. See you soon, Iona."

Oh, fuck off psycho so I can save your wife and myself from your clutches.

"Take care. Tim. I can't wait to get to Switzerland!"

Antonio grunted, and they both went outside. I breathed out a huge sigh. I was alone at last and needed to be sure they were gone.

I heard a car engine start, then another. I listened to a car pulling away, and a few seconds later, the other vehicle went. I tried to imagine the time it would take them to go down the drive and turn onto the main road.

I closed my eyes. I needed to reset. I sat on the sofa and took five long breaths in and out. I needed to focus. I wouldn't win this in a state of hysteria.

Once I was satisfied they were gone, it was time to face the music with Tim's wife, Jess.

Tim said he tied her up. I searched around to find scissors or something to cut her free.

I raked about in a drawer and found a big pair of scissors. It was lucky I hadn't seen them earlier; I might have tried to attack Tim and Antonio to escape. I know that would've been a foolish idea and most likely to have ended badly.

I approached the door and hesitated. Should I knock and give Jess a warning that I was coming in?

I decided to go in. It was pitch dark, and only the light from the open door was bleeding in.

I fumbled on the wall for a light switch and found one. On came a weak light in the centre of the ceiling. It was one of those depressing bulbs that gave off a dismal light, and no light shade was attached.

I heard a feeble yelp from the far corner. I looked over. There was Jess. I felt so bad. She was sitting on the concrete floor. There were no floor coverings in here. They had tied her wrist to a steel pole and put duct tape over her mouth. I could see she'd been crying. Her eyes had a terrified look. This poor woman didn't deserve any of this. I couldn't take in how appalling this was and how Tim thought it was okay. He was a madman.

I thought I'd better explain the plan to Jess before I removed the duct tape. As soon as I removed it, all hell could break loose. It was cruel not to release her immediately, but I needed to make the best use of our time and explain what we needed to do without interruptions.

"Jess, I'm here to help you. I'm sorry I've devastated your life, and I'll do my utmost to make amends to you." I said sincerely. "I'm about to remove this tape from your mouth and cut the ropes free, but please listen to me, as we don't have much time. Do you understand?"

Jess nodded, her eyes stopped glaring at me, but she looked almost relieved.

I continued,

"We're about a 45-minute drive from Bellagio. Outside, to the right of the building, is a stream and a wooded area. We need to make a run for it and try not to leave a trail of what direction we have gone in. If, for any reason, we are split up, you make sure you run and keep running along the stream until you find somewhere you can call for help."

Jess nodded again.

"I don't want to scare you, but Tim intends to leave you here without help or let anyone know where you are. He thinks I'm going along with his mental plan to go with him to Switzerland, but I'm only pretending to get both of us out of here. He's returned to the hotel to collect my belongings, and Antonio has gone to collect his wife. We have two hours to create some distance and get help or hide until we can. Is this all clear to you?"

Jess nodded.

I put my hand over and gently tugged the duct tape away. Jess gasped and coughed. I cut the ropes to free her hands and gave her some water.

She started crying, "I can't believe what he's done to me, what you've both done!"

"I'm so sorry," I said again.

"I deserve all that is coming to me, but you don't. You deserve to get safely back to your daughter. Can we agree to pick this up again later when we're in safety?"

I hoped she would say yes; this was no time for a wife and mistress argument.

Jess nodded.

"Yes, fuck that bastard, there is no way he's getting away with this!"

"That is more like it!" I said encouragingly. "Right, we've both got trainers on, which is a plus. Are you injured at all?"

"I don't think so," replied Jess, "just a bit dehydrated."

"Right, we'll get more water on the way out, there is a fridge that big fat Antonio has stocked up with water."

We returned to the lounge room, and I headed to the fridge. It was full of water and beer.

"Right, two bottles each should get us where we need to go," I said, "and one to leave a trail in the wrong direction!"

Jess looked at me.

"I've been suggesting to Tim that there are great buildings to hide in across the yard. So, when they return, I want them to think we're hiding. Let us drop a couple of things and an empty water bottle. I'll drop my scarf near an outbuilding door, and we'll splash some water too. It might buy us extra time."

Then I had a thought,

"I'm assuming you don't have your phone?"

"Correct," he took it off me and launched it into the lake!"

"Arsehole," I said.

We both managed a small giggle. It was weird to share a joke with the estranged wife in such dire circumstances.

"Okay, let's get moving," I continued.

I led the way to the door and then gently opened it. I was glad when it opened, but it hadn't occurred to me that they could have locked us in. It was still light. Luckily, my watch was on, so I knew we still had time. It is a pity it wasn't my Apple Watch, then I could have alerted someone.

I peeked outside, left and right. It was silent. There were no cars and no signs of anyone. I was confident we were alone.

"Stay here until I signal to you, " I told Jess.

I ran across the yard toward the faraway building and dropped my scarf at the edge. I then poured out the water from the bottle and left the empty bottle lying near the scarf. I was sure they would notice it.

I ran back to the house to get Jess. She came out, and we started to run towards the stream and the wooded area. Suddenly, I heard a car. It sounded as if it was coming up the road towards the buildings.

Jess heard it too; she looked alarmed.

"Shit," I said, "keep running I don't think they will see us as the building they park beside in will obstruct their view.

Soon, we reached the stream. In the middle, there were a couple of handy stepping stones. We quickly hopped over them and into the trees on the other side. There were bushes too.

"Get behind here just now, just till I see who has returned," I told Jess.

From our viewpoint, I could see the building we had been in. Then I saw a car. It wasn't Tim's, so I knew it wasn't him. A woman got out, and I saw Antonio get out on the other side.

"Fuck, he was quick," I said startled. I saw him walk over toward where I had left the scarf. I realised Antonio hadn't said how far away he had to drive to collect his wife; he just said he would return by 6.30 pm.

This was an error on my part for not considering this!

"This is our chance, Jess. Go this way, start running and don't stop until I tell you to."

Jess dived out and started to run, followed by me. I decided not to look back. It wouldn't be long before Antonio entered the building and realised we were gone. Then he would phone Tim. The good news was that Antonio, and his wife didn't look like they could run the length of themselves. If it had been Tim, he was a fast runner in a running club, so I was thankful it wasn't him.

Jess was a good runner, too. She was ahead of me, so I decided to keep her pace. We ran through the woods, following the stream. Then I could see we were coming to a clearing, but I also noticed the stream had led us close to the main road.

There was a risk of Tim driving back down and seeing us, or Antonio going back out in the car to look for us.

"Jess, stop before the edge of the woods, don't run into the clearing," I shouted ahead.

Jess came to a halt. We both took time to catch our breaths and drink some water.

"I feel like I'm in an episode of survival," I joked, "what a way to spend a Monday afternoon in Italy."

Jess laughed, too. The relief that we had put some distance between us and them was palpable.

"Right, what is the plan now?" asked Jess. "I'm determined to get home to my daughter and be free of that fucking control freak!" she declared.

Control freak, it sounded like she had a time of it with Tim. Why didn't I see that he was a wolf in sheep's clothing? I reckoned

I didn't see it as I wasn't looking for him as a partner, just a playmate. Also, he was having an affair, so this should've dawned on me before now. I couldn't get into this; we had to concentrate on getting help.

"I'll make sure you do, Jess," I said, "it's the least I can do!"

We recovered from the first run. I looked across the clearing. It was about 200m to the next set of trees. We needed to leave the stream as it headed down to the road.

I knew going on the road would mean a chance to get help, but I couldn't risk it. Antonio or Tim could come along at any time.

"Right," I said to Jess, "we can make that next set of trees in about 5 minutes. We can't go on the road in case Antonio is out looking for us."

Jess agreed. We set off at a good pace. I was so thankful Jess had a proficient level of fitness.

We made it across with some near misses on the bumpy terrain. Injured ankles were the last thing we needed right now.

Jess let out a squeal.

"What's wrong?" I asked, my heart thumping.

"No, it's okay. There is a house up ahead."

I felt relieved. Hopefully, the owner would be in. We could call for help. I looked at my watch. It was now 5:15 pm From what we could see, the house was set back from the main road. We could approach from behind and hide in the trees until we almost reached it. It looked like there was a fence up around the garden.

It didn't take us long until we reached the back garden gate. We decided we would go round the front as it may scare the owners with strangers appearing in their back garden. We followed the fence around and reached the front door. I hoped someone was in. We knocked on the door and stood back waiting for a reply.

"Oh, you think you're smart, do you?" said a voice behind. I spun around, and there was Tim standing. He was pointing a gun at us.

I froze on the spot.

Jess let out a cry.

He now knew I had tricked him.

Fuck!

"Antonio saw you heading to the woods. I knew this place was the next one along, so I reckoned I could find you both easily, and here we are! So predictable!" he said menacingly.

"Tim," I said, trying to sound authoritative. "Have you taken leave of your senses? You're standing there pointing a fucking gun at the mother of your child and me. How the fuck is that going to solve anything."

Just then, the front door opened, and a man and woman in their sixties stood there, looking puzzled.

Then they saw Tim with the gun, and they looked shaken.

"I think we'll all go inside," said Tim, pointing the gun to indicate we should move in.

This was fucking ridiculous. There were four of us and one of him. I wondered if Tim had even loaded the gun, but I wasn't taking any chances. We now had two strangers involved who were probably cooking their dinner in the kitchen when we brought this bedlam up on them!

Now, I was sick of this fucking plan of his. I caught Jess's eye from the side and gave her a nod, hoping she'd realise I had a plan. She looked as if she noticed my vibe; I hoped she did.

I was thinking that mad psycho face would've shot us already if he were going to. He was undecided about how to move forward. However, this was shocking now that he had involved two strangers in the situation. They could identify him even if I managed to talk Tim into taking Jess and me to Switzerland. Then we could escape by hiking back over the Alps. I had seen it all in the movies; however, it was very different when it happened to you!

The man had put his arm around his wife. She was crying quietly. No wonder, a bloody arsehole with a gun had just violated their ideal living space in the Italian countryside. What a mess!

I suddenly longed to see Mike and hug him. Although I had only known him briefly, it felt like a lifetime.

"Sit down," Tim instructed us all.

Well, at least we weren't kneeling on the floor with our hands behind our heads yet!

There were two big sofas. So, we all sat down. What now? I focused on the room. There were plenty of ornaments and vases.

Weapons!

"So, Iona," Tim said as if he were a school principal, "why did you think you could get away with this?"

"Get away with what, Tim? My freedom?"

My answer phased Tim. He was so engaged in his plan that he must have convinced himself that what he was doing was normal.

"Jess, you shouldn't have come here. It is your fault you're in this situation. You're such an idiot. You know I know best," he said, looking at Jess.

Fucking hell, he was an absolute fruitcake.

"I think you'll find the only idiot in the room is you!" Jess exclaimed.

I could tell Jess hadn't stood up to him before, but she must have felt so pissed with him at that moment. Also, there was safety in numbers, and she usually had to deal with him alone. I was proud of her stance even though he was pointing a gun at us.

Tim looked shocked when Jess gave him back his type of medicine. He was acting irrationally and was thrown by these responses. Did he expect us to sit there like quivering wrecks?

"Tim," I said. "This couple has nothing to do with this. Take Jess and me back to where we were. I can drive, and you can hold a gun to my head while I drive."

"Oh, here you go, Iona. Do you think I'm going to trust a single thing you say? You cheated on me with Mike, then lied to me, saying you would go to Switzerland!"

He was getting mad. A madman with a gun wasn't suitable for negotiations.

"Where is Antonio?" I asked to change the direction of the conversation.

"He is waiting on us with his wife," Tim replied.

"Well, what are you going to do then?" I asked.

He looked unsure of how to reply.

"Wouldn't it be better just to go and meet him? We can leave Jess and this couple here; we'll be in Switzerland anyway."

I thought if we could get him between us, we might have a chance to disarm him. He had us all sitting targets on the sofas, with a gun in our faces. Still, I wasn't sure the gun was loaded.

I noticed the clock on the wall. It was 5.45 pm My boys would soon know I was missing. I wouldn't show up for dinner at six as arranged. However, they had no way of knowing where I was.

"Did you get my stuff from the hotel?" I asked Tim.

"Some of it," he replied, "then Antonio called me to say you had run off. Why couldn't you go along with the plan, Iona? I saw your ex-husband sitting in the lounge. He called me over, but I just waved and left!"

Oh, that was good news to me. Keith would be indignant about this. He would then think about it and think it was strange that Tim didn't go over and talk to him. This renewed my hope that something was happening in the background. My ex-husband was judgmental and had already formed an opinion about Tim, which may help Jess and me. I could only hope.

I could see Tim was thinking and trying to work out what his best move was. I thought he was a stupid idiot who hadn't really thought this through. The couple in question could now have him charged with holding them at gunpoint. On top of this, he'd kidnapped Jess and me. However, considering he was also acting like a mad psychopath, I didn't want to endanger the lives of three other people by guessing how he might react. I couldn't have predicted this situation, in which we found ourselves.

"Okay," he said as if we had all decided to order a takeaway. "We'll go, Iona, but first you need to help me tie these three up so they can't call for help.'"

What?

I wanted to strangle him. He was serious. He wanted me to tie people up. Then I thought this might give me some time.

"So, what exactly should I use to tie them up?" I asked.

He had a rucksack on his shoulders, which I hadn't noticed in all the chaos. He shrugged it off one shoulder while still pointing the gun at us, and then he worked it off his other shoulder. I felt he had watched too many TV dramas, as well, where stuff like this happened.

"Open it," he demanded, "there is rope inside."

I stared at him for a moment. He had brought rope and was determined to get his way.

I fumbled in the bag, trying to see if there was anything I could use as a weapon or at least pass on to Jess. I felt something mental, probably a pen knife. I took the rope and pen knife together, hoping he wouldn't see I had it.

"The rope is already cut into lengths," he said, "Just untie it and you'll see."

Sure enough, I untied the middle knot, and several lengths of rope fell on the floor. I was glad Tim had cut up the ropes; at least he couldn't hang anyone!

I decided to tie the couple up first and then try to slip the pen knife while I was tying Jess up.

"I'm so sorry about this," I apologised to the man. I decided to tie him up first as he was the most likely to show bravado, which could end in tragedy. His wife started crying. I hated Tim for this, terrifying people who had no part of his stupid fucking plan.

"It's okay," I reassured the lady. We'll be gone soon, then you'll be safe." I hoped she understood me.

"See what you've caused, Iona," Tim stated.

I swung around. Although I was happy, he was disturbed by the woman's distress!

He was still pointing the gun and glaring at me. He believed I was the one upsetting this couple in their own home while he held a gun to them.

I wanted to run at and throttle him for his arrogance and stupidity. I'm glad I managed to hold back, as it could get messy. I decided to say nothing at all.

I quietly tied up the man's hands behind his back, then the woman's. Then it was Jess's turn.

She looked at me, and I made signs with my eyes. I had managed to put the pen knife in my pocket. I was behind the sofa.

"Tim, I thought I saw lights!" I exclaimed. He turned around to look out the window, and I quickly slipped the knife into Jess's hand, which was behind her back. The man saw me do it and gave me a quick nod of understanding.

Tim spun back around.

"Right, they're all tied up," I said. Do you want me to do their feet, too? There is enough rope."

I was hoping he would say yes, as that would give people more time to miss me and come looking.

"For fuck's sake, Iona," Tim said, "that's too far"!

Jess and I both let out a laugh of disbelief.

He looked displeased that we were in harmony.

"Right, Iona, let's go!" Tim demanded.

I could see a vase on the sideboard that I would need to pass. If Tim walked before me, I would have the chance to grab it.

"Tim, can we quit with the pointing a gun at me now?" I questioned, "This is hardly a romantic way to start a new life in Switzerland with you pointing a gun in my face."

It was a long shot, but he took the gun and put it in his jeans' waistband.

I smiled. "That is better."

I knew not to do anything hasty. Slow and sure was the key here. He lifted his rucksack and made a move to the door. He was letting me go behind him. Fantastic, I loved what a stupid arsehole he was.

I grabbed the vase and whammed him over the head with it. He let out a cry and dropped to the floor. I got down beside him and wiggled the gun out of his waistband. I wasn't sure how long he would stay unconscious. I was glad I hadn't killed him; I certainly wasn't doing time for murdering this idiot.

Jess was already cutting her ropes with the pen knife. I released the couple, and the man motioned that we could tie Tim up with the ropes. This was a great idea. Tim groaned, so we had to get to work quickly.

Just at this moment, there was a knock at the door. Jess ran to answer it.

I tried to call her to tell her not to answer the door until we checked who it was when she walked back into the room. Her face looked like she had seen a ghost, then behind her came Antonio with a gun pointed at her back.

Fucking hell, I couldn't believe it. We had nearly escaped, and now we were back to square one. I glanced around the room. The man had disappeared. The woman sat on the couch, looking anxious. My heart raced. Had the man managed to get out the back and escape to call for help?

Then suddenly, he came from behind Antonio. There must have been another hallway that led back around from the kitchen to the front of the house. The man knocked Antonio out with a large iron frying pan. Antonio fell forward, knocking into Jess. Jess squealed as she fell forward. Luckily, she managed to step forward simultaneously and landed on the sofa, while Antonio landed on the floor. The gun had flown from his hand and spun across the room.

We all looked at each other, relieved. Luckily, the man had the clever idea to go around in a circle to get behind Antonio. It's easier if you know the layout of a house. Thank goodness for the residents!

"Let's all get out of here," I shouted out. We'd not tied them up, but I wanted out of there fast. The man shook his head and pointed at the ropes. He was right; we all needed to tie these two up.

There was another knock at the door. Fuck this place was busy.

I motioned to everyone to keep quiet. Then I pointed at Antonio and mouthed silently that it could be his wife with him. The man understood what I meant and pointed towards the back of the house and the back door.

We quietly moved towards the back door; then I felt a hand grab my ankle. Antonio had stirred. I kicked like a mad woman and freed myself, then made out after the others. However, I didn't have time to grab either of the guns that lay on the floor.

The man indicated that we head to the trees. Back in the direction from which Jess and I had come earlier. He had weaponised himself with a shotgun. At least that was some form of protection.

We started running back across the field. We kept running and reached the trees.

We heard shots ring out, and a woman's voice called out, speaking in Italian. I didn't know what she said but knew it was Antonio's wife.

Next, I heard a roar: "IONA. " It was Tim's voice: "You're not going to get away!"

Why the fuck did he have to gain consciousness?

I started to feel that the man may have been ex-military. He quickly organised us to get behind him and hide, while he kept in front of us, also hidden from view.

We could see Antonio and his wife crossing the field with guns. Although we heard Tim call out, we couldn't see him.

The man signalled to us to remain quiet. I wanted to run, but he seemed to know what he was doing. Antonio and his wife must've thought we had returned to the woods toward the buildings again. Instead of approaching us, they headed to the left, away from us. This must have been the man's plan. He signalled to us to stay where we were. We were all aware there was no sign of Tim yet.

We all stood still, anxious to make our next move to safety.

Suddenly, someone grabbed me from behind and put a hand over my mouth.

"You bitch, Iona, you fucking bitch," Tim said menacingly into my ear. I could feel the metal of the gun pointed at my forehead.

I was terrified, but he was getting none of my terror. I was beyond pissed off with him!

Jess and the couple turned around, horrified.

"Right, back to the house, the lot of you," Tim demanded. "You drop the gun he told the man."

I could see the man weigh the option of taking a shot at Tim, but he put the gun on the grass. He must've decided it was risky, and he might shoot me instead.

The other three walked back in front in silence. I was held behind with Tim's grip and a gun to my head.

I was weighing up if I could take him on, wrestle him down, and shoot him, but that was a far-fetched idea. I was between fear and rage. I couldn't believe what an animal Tim had turned into. I still wasn't entirely convinced it was a loaded gun; however, this thought had to lie for now. I wasn't letting Tim shoot me. He was a raving lunatic.

From the corner of my eye, I saw blue flashing lights. Hope instantly returned to my heart. Help was on its way. Tim didn't react. He was too busy in his crazed mind, taking me hostage and keeping me as his prize forever, the prick. I hoped the police would turn off the blue lights before Tim saw them. I hoped the others wouldn't react or alert Tim.

They kept walking, but I noticed them all glance at each other.

"Don't get any funny ideas," Tim shouted at them. Good; he hadn't seen the lights. He thought they were plotting to escape.

I had no idea how this would play out. I felt mental and physical exhaustion, but I had to keep going. I wanted to see my boys, I wanted to see Mike.

As we approached the house, a voice suddenly called out from a megaphone. "We have you surrounded, please drop your weapon."

This startled Tim and temporarily threw him off guard. I heard the gun drop on the grass. This was my chance; I threw my leg behind me as hard as possible and kicked him hard on the shin. He yelped, letting go of me, and I shoved him over and kicked him hard in the balls. He howled, and I took to my heels and ran like the wind.

I ran as fast as I could, not knowing what the others were doing. I think I shouted, "Run."

I was running, but suddenly someone scooped me up. My feet rose from the ground. I kicked, squealed, and fought. Tim had caught me again!

"Let me go, let me go you fucking nutcase," I called out hysterically. I was struggling to escape. My heart was beating out of my chest.

"Iona, it's me, Iona, you're safe." I couldn't believe the voice; it was Mike. I opened my eyes and looked at him.

"What kept you?" I asked.

Then I kissed him like I had never kissed anyone before.

"Mum, Mum, are you okay?" Dan and Jack came running forward.

"Looks like she's fine!" said Dan sarcastically.

I stopped kissing Mike, and he let me down from his arms to hug my boys.

Then Keith and Sandra appeared. "Fuck, I'm even pleased to see you two," I said.

They laughed and both said at the same time, "To be fair we're fucking pleased to see you too!"

Then we all laughed. Jess then appeared; thank goodness she was okay too.

"The man and woman?" I asked her. She nodded and smiled; they were fine, too.

Then, all of us did this once-only, never-to-be-repeated team hug. It would've been the most awkward hug at any other time, but for now, it was great and comforting.

Next, Tim appeared handcuffed, escorted by two police officers. We were all standing at the front of the house as he was marched past into a car. He glared at me, and I glared right back. In the car, I could see Antonio and his wife looking angry.

I wanted to know how they had found us.

Mike explained that the police had released the skipper and him late in the afternoon. As the news had spread about what had happened and Antonio's alleged disappearance, people started to report to the police that they'd seen Antonio. The police had also uncovered Antonio's criminal activities. Informants made them aware that Antonio might have old buildings in the countryside that he used.

They watched his house and discovered him coming back to collect his wife. Then they decided to follow him to see where he went. At this point, they were unaware that Antonio and Tim had kidnapped Jess and me.

So, they observed Antonio and his wife's movements from afar. They wouldn't have seen Jess and me from the road when we ran for freedom.

Then Tim had appeared at the hotel and acted strangely in front of Keith. Just after Tim left the hotel, Ispettore Colombo appeared with Mike and the skipper to update everyone on what was happening. He told them they had Antonio under observation. Keith sent my boys to my bedroom to fetch me and discovered I was missing, along with my laptop and some belongings. At the same time, the police following Antonio and his wife put out a call for urgent, armed backup to the couple's house as they had followed Antonio there and seen his wife getting out of the car with a gun. It wasn't clear how Tim managed to find the house Jess and I ran to, but the police would find out when they interviewed Tim.

We'd all been quick off the mark to run into the woods and hide, but the officers had to wait for backup before proceeding.

By this point, all my gang, including Mike, decided they were coming to the rescue too.

So, here we all were. I then saw the man and woman talking to Ispettore Colombo. I walked over and gave them a huge hug. "Grazie!" I said.

The man and woman smiled, glad the ordeal was over. The man could speak a little English. He told me he had been in the army when he was younger and hadn't had this much excitement in a long time, then laughed. His wife laughed too.

Thank fuck they had a sense of humour. Jess and I had dragged them into a drama that could've turned out very nasty.

I looked over and saw Jess sitting on the front wall of the property. She was on the phone, so I waited until she came off.

"I don't know what to say to you," I said. I didn't have a clue what to say. I had lost a lover whom I was intending to move on from anyway, whereas she had learned that her husband, the father of her daughter, was having an affair and was now a lunatic.

"Iona, I don't know what to say either. My daughter is safe at home, so that is the only thing I want to know right now. I thought he might have been keeping her somewhere, too! Can we meet tomorrow to talk this through? I want a bath, dinner, and sleep."

"Sounds like a plan," I said meekly.

Keith and Sandra approached and offered to take Jess and the boys back to the hotel in their hired car, for which I was grateful.

Ispettore Colombo said he would take statements from us all in the morning.

I promised the boys I was following right behind them back to the hotel and waved them off.

Mike came over.

"I never thought meeting you would be better than a movie set," he laughed. "You certainly know how to keep a man on his toes!"

"Mike," I don't know where to begin. I'm so sorry you were dragged into my disaster!" I said.

He smiled, "Come here!" Then he hugged me close and just held me. It was blissful.

After a long, satisfying hug, he said, "You're coming back to the hotel for a nice hot bath, which I'm going to run for you!"

"I suppose I'll have to obey then," I said with a twinkle in my eye. I was so happy he wasn't running away from the bedlam.

"I can't believe you're so cool about this," I said gratefully.

"I'll tell you why," he smiled, "the note you gave to Ispettore Colombo to give me. It melted my heart. You went the extra mile to try to save me. How were you supposed to know how events would unfold? It isn't your fault, Iona."

Then he hugged and kissed me again. Ispettore Colombo coughed and offered us a lift back to Bellagio.

Chapter 25

I don't think I've ever had such a good sleep in my entire life. When we returned to the hotel, I had the warmest bath, Mike came in it with me, and we soaked blissfully in the bubbles. I remember getting out, and he rubbed me dry, then put a soft cotton bathrobe on me and carried me over to the bed.

The next thing I knew, it was morning. I still wore the robe, and Mike was lying beside me with his arm over me. He was gorgeous, even asleep. My heart skipped a beat.

Then everything came flooding back. It was unbelievable.

Mike stirred.

"Good morning, gorgeous Iona," he smiled.

"Good morning, marvellous Mike," I giggled back.

Then I looked at him thoughtfully.

"Mike, I need to go and find Jess and speak to her."

Mike nodded, "I know. Take your time. You both probably have a lot to talk about."

He hugged me and kissed me on the forehead, then I quickly got ready and headed downstairs.

I wasn't usually nervous, but I was full of anxiety. I knew Jess and I had worked together the day before to escape. However, that was an adrenaline-filled situation.

Now, a day later, she would've had time to think about the weekend's events. I couldn't believe it was Tuesday morning. By now, I was supposed to be back at work. Work, I hadn't even thought about it. I would need to call in. However, I expected my colleagues to have seen the news over the last two days.

Jess was sitting on the sofa by the windows, looking over the lake. I was glad Jess was there, so I didn't need to search for her.

I approached gingerly. How would I start this conversation?

Jess looked up and smiled; I was grateful for this. I sat down on the sofa across from her.

"I don't know where to start, to be honest, Jess," I admitted.

"I've been awake all night pondering this," replied Jess. "I relived Saturday into Sunday morning when I knew Tim was acting strangely. He has always been in charge of our relationship, being bossy to my daughter and me, but on Saturday night, he acted like an injured puppy dog. He was constantly looking at his phone. He took a couple of calls and said it was work. I knew it wasn't work as he never worked weekends. He had been acting weird since Friday when Lara injured her arm. I thought perhaps he was worried about her. Let me clarify, he's bossy, but he isn't physically abusive."

I nodded and let Jess continue.

"I now know he was weird because he had a big plan to run away. He must have been torn between not giving the game away, and I think he genuinely cares about Lara. However, I'm unsure if he intended for her to come and live with you and him in Switzerland once you settled there!

Anyway, he was so agitated, and he was marching about the lounge. By this time, it was midnight, and Lara was asleep. He went to the toilet and left his phone on the table, so I was able to have a quick look. Well, there was a whole drama exploding before my eyes. I could hardly take it in. The deceit was overwhelming. Love messages to you, messages to Antonio, I could scarcely breathe."

My stomach churned hearing this from Jess. The poor woman was finding out, and I was one of the guilty parties.

"He came back from the toilet, and I was sitting there. He stopped dead in his tracks, obviously reeling at seeing me with his phone. He wasn't at all remorseful, though. He said I would've found out soon anyway and grabbed the phone from me.

He said you were in danger and needed to see your boys before heading to Lake Como. As if he was telling me he was going to the shop for a fucking newspaper."

This story was getting worse and worse. What a prick Tim was! How awful was I for being part of it?

Jess continued, "I couldn't speak, as no words would come. I was in shock. At first, I aimed my rage at you, Iona. I started to get mad; I smashed vases and ornaments against the wall. But Tim, no, he wasn't one ounce bothered. He was collecting his passport and packing an overnight bag. Lara heard the commotion and came downstairs crying."

Shit, I could hardly bare to hear all this, but I had to listen!

"So, he announces he's going to Glasgow to talk to your boys, then catching a flight to Milan. And I thought, is that fucking right, I'll be on the plane to fucking Milan too and have it out with this bitch!"

I cringed.

"I phoned his mother. The news about Tim's actions shocked her. She has always been nice; he bossed her about as well. We had to do things Tim's way or no way. I was crying, then angry. She headed straight over to our house. She told me Tim's dad had treated her the same way, and she couldn't stand by any longer and let her granddaughter and daughter-in-law suffer. She booked us all on a flight to Milan for Sunday. Tim must have caught an earlier flight, as we didn't see him at the airport. I knew he was coming to Bellagio, and he used my booking.com account to book a taxi from Milan to Bellagio. Silly bastard."

I looked at Jess apologetically; I was so sorry about all this. She wanted to speak more.

"By the time we arrived here, there was such a commotion on the news about it all. So, we could see things had gotten profoundly serious. People were missing; the police were involved. I was still shocked that my bossy husband, whom I thought I loved, was dragging my daughter and me into this turmoil. I was still furious about you, Iona."

I understood why!

"Then there you were standing, and blind rage ensued, and I just came right at you and knocked you out. I've never been in a physical fight in my life, so I couldn't believe how hard I punched you."

"I bet it felt good, though!" I managed to say.

Jess let out a laugh, "Yes, for a moment it did, but then I thought I had killed you, and I was traumatised. Then they pulled me away from you. Tim was raging with me. I could see he was apoplectic. He didn't ask how I was and shoved me out of the way to get to you. This is when I realised he didn't love me, and I wondered if he ever had."

My heart sank. Imagine me causing someone's heartache. I made a mental note to myself never to do anything like this again.

"Then the events unfolding were so shocking. After I had punched you, Ispettore Colombo told me I would need to stay in Bellagio until you regained consciousness, and they would tell me if you wanted to charge me, Iona. At this point, I didn't care. Then, I looked at Lara and knew I had to screw my head on for her sake. Tim wanted nothing to do with me; he told Lara everything would be okay. Then he gave his mother a row for helping us come to Bellagio.

I knew he was bossy, but I never knew he was so mean. Perhaps I always knew when I reflect on our life together."

Jess was laying her heart on her sleeve here. I couldn't interrupt.

"The rest you probably know. I agreed his mum could take Lara home and hoped

Tim and I could talk it through at least. Next thing I know, I woke up tied to a pipe with Tim standing over me, telling me I'd wasted his plans! By this point, I was no longer sad or interested in being near him. I was thinking you were welcome to have him. Then I heard you all talking in the room next door. I must admit, Iona, you're a great actor. I was sure you were following his plan, and I was thinking what a cow you were.

I thought you came into the room to gloat over me. I was shocked when you said you were going to help me. I knew I had to try and trust you as I couldn't see how else I would escape. I'm glad I did. Somewhere between that room and the finale of us running away, I stopped hating you. I don't think we can be friends, but my relationship wasn't enjoyable, and the escape from it feels great. I just kept going along with it, like a bad habit. You impressed me with your strength, going to great lengths to save me. It was a pleasant surprise in the middle of the mayhem.

I'm not letting you off the hook for having an affair with my husband, as I could have been a happily married woman. You didn't care about that, but I'm glad to be free of him. Until Saturday night, I didn't know that was what I desired."

Jess had said all the things I reckoned she would say. I was digesting everything she said. She was correct, at the time, I didn't give a damn about the consequences of my actions having an affair with Tim.

"Jess, you're brave considering the shocking weekend you've been through. You're correct when you say I didn't care. I'm sorry I was that person. It may not be consolation, but I promise I've learned an extremely valuable lesson that will never leave me. Seeing you and Lara as real people makes me incredibly ashamed of my actions. I should've considered this initially, but I've never been involved with Tim.

I know this may not be much, but Tim was also interested in me, as I invested a lot of money. So, he wanted me to use this money to set up his planned new life for us. I convinced him to go to the hotel and fetch my laptop. I'll give you and Lara money to start afresh. Please accept it with my sincere apologies."

Jess considered what I offered and nodded her head in agreement. "A helping hand is a weight off my mind; I wondered where to start. I know you're not bad, but please promise to consider other people in the future."

"I promise!" I said, and I meant it.

Just at that, I glimpsed the whole gang coming over. Keith with Sandra, then

Jack and Dan. Behind them was Mr Drop Dead Gorgeous himself, Mike.

"Are secret agents finished here?" asked Mike.

Jess and I giggled like schoolchildren and nodded.

"Great," he said. You'll all be guests at my house party on Friday. Jess, your mother-in-law, will head back over with your daughter! Iona, I've told your employer you're convalescing at my house for a week after your ordeal. The rest of you can stay here as my guests until Monday.

Jack and Dan's faces were a picture of delight. "Really?" they said at the same time.

"Yes, guys," replied Mike, we all need fun after all the bedlam.

Keith and Sandra looked stunned. They didn't know what to say. Then, together, they said, "Thank you!"

I was beginning to think they were pretty cute, but it was probably the bang to my head.

Jess looked excited and nodded her head in agreement.

I wasn't protesting at all. A week with Mike at his villa.

Yes, please!

"Brilliant," said Mike, "all sorted, let us all have brunch to celebrate."

Chapter 26

The following day was a mix of emotions. We were still reeling from an adrenaline-filled weekend, and the realisation of the events slowly hit home. We all ended up staying at the hotel. Mike and I hadn't ventured back to the villa, as the party preparations were in full swing, and we decided it was better to let Emilio get on with it.

The delayed shock came in waves, like an aftershock. It crept up on me when I wasn't looking. Shivers ran down my spine every time I imagined how lucky Jess and I were to escape.

The inspector visited to update us. The Italian police dealt with Tim and Antonio, and the UK police were involved with Tim as well. I had to speak to the UK police about Tim and explain everything that had happened.

Mike was a rock by my side, holding my hand. He gave me much-needed hugs at the right time.

All the while, he was getting unwanted press attention about the drama. You know, the news shows on television that twist and turn stories in any way they can, trying to make something out of nothing.

The conspiracy theories were hot on the trail. People appeared on video link on daytime news, trying to make elaborate efforts to place Mike as the guilty party. Even though the suspected murder victim, Antonio, was alive and locked up in jail.

It was exhausting. The unrelenting narrative played on TV all day on Wednesday. Mike tried to keep a bright outlook, but I could see this was wearing him down, too.

Jess visited Tim at the jail to tell him exactly what she thought of him. The police advised against this, but she did it anyway.

She returned on Wednesday night looking exhausted but also satisfied and unburdened, as if she had gotten everything out of her system.

I asked her if she wanted to talk about it. She said she had gone to close the chapter of her life with Tim. To confirm what she already thought of him for his actions. She wanted to look into his eyes and tell him that far from ruining her life, she would now enjoy a freedom she had forgotten existed. She said the downtrodden woman he had made her was gone. She said he had no remorse at all. He was still angry and referred to me as 'that bitch Iona' who ruined everything for him. She enjoyed telling me this, which was fair in the circumstances. However, she said she told him I did the decent thing, saving her instead of him. To which he started shouting abuse at her and she told him to 'fuck off' and left.

I never wanted to set eyes on Tim again. However, the police told me a trial would happen if Tim didn't plead guilty, so I was unsure if I would get my wish.

It was strange to think that a week ago, I liked Tim enough to come for a weekend to Bellagio with total disregard for his family or mine. Now, he was an alien to me, someone I didn't know had lurked beneath the guy I had sex with once a week.

I found it hard to forgive myself for my role in this fiasco. All these people were involved, and I had turned their lives upside down.

However, later on Wednesday evening, Mike gathered us all together.

"My lawyers are speaking to the media about defamation of character, so they will all shut up soon. And as far as I know, no publicity is bad publicity. The police have everything else under control here. So, we'll all cheer up for tomorrow and go water skiing?" He winked at me, "I already promised Iona this on Saturday afternoon. It seems like such a long time ago!"

"Oh, we can't water ski, we don't know how to!" Keith and Sandra spoke at the same time.

We all burst out laughing.

"There'll be an instructor," Mike smiled at them, "I think you two might end up being the best at it!"

They both held each other's hands, giggling. I thought they were cute for a second time. What was wrong with me?

Of course, Jack and Dan were buzzing.

"Mum, this is brilliant! We have been in three movies since Saturday night, from horror to romance to adventure!" Dan stated.

I threw a cushion at him.

We all laughed again, and normality flowed back to us. I felt the difference, and the burden started to shift.

Jess's mother-in-law had told her to stay in Bellagio to keep informed about what was happening with Tim and to keep her in the loop. She said Lara was doing well and didn't know everything, so she would keep her in the UK and shield her from the spotlight. She told Jess to attend Mike's party on Friday and enjoy herself, as she needed fun and respite after what Tim had done to her.

"I would bloody love to go water skiing" Jess joined in, "I deserve a good fucking laugh!"

We all laughed in agreement.

Chapter 27

Once everyone had gone to bed, Mike and I were alone. We went up to our room. He had a wild look in his eye, and I started to get excited.

"Sunday was a long time ago," he growled, "the werewolf is hungry!"

I shrieked excitedly as he scooped me up in his arms and threw me onto the bed like a wild animal. I didn't want to protest, but I was in the mood to play.

I pretended to try to get away by rolling to the side. Mike pulled me back.

"Where do you think you're going?" he said, his voice intense and wild.

I stared at him, my eyes on fire. I wanted to feel all his strength. He grabbed my chin and kissed my mouth roughly. I loved it, but I slapped his face.

"What's the werewolf going to do about that?" I asked tauntingly.

Oh, I wanted to succumb so much, but loved this delayed pleasure.

Mike firmly grabbed my hair to show me he wanted to be in charge. Glaring into my eyes like a man possessed. He ripped open my blouse, kissed my mouth and neck as if he were devouring me.

I screamed out in joy.

Then again, I wrestled to escape. I was loving this, and I knew he was too. I feel his hard cock under his shorts.

He tried to hold me still, but I escaped onto the floor. He gave me a couple of seconds, then came down after me.

Then he grabbed me from behind.

"Just the way I want you," he growled.

I couldn't resist anymore!

He bent me over the side of the bed and tore down my knickers with one hand, expertly holding me in place with the other. The he released his hard cock from his shorts and entered me.

It was fast and furious, ecstatic, and crazy. I squealed out, and he groaned. We were like wild animals mating, primal and fierce.

He pulled my body up from the bed, still shagging me from behind, grabbing my tits in his hands.

My back pressed against his chest. His mouth was beside my ear. He breathed heavily with the energy he was expelling. Our bodies are sweating, merging into one.

It was explosive, and then we crashed beside each other on the floor, saying nothing and gazing into each other's eyes.

Utter satisfaction!

After about 10 minutes, Mike spoke,

"I hope these walls are soundproof,"

And we both laughed hysterically.

Chapter 28

We were up early the next morning. We made our way to the jetty where the skipper awaited us. I didn't realise he was our instructor. Mike kept that a secret. He knowingly grinned at me; we had all escaped the bedlam. I blushed thinking of what he might have seen Mike and me getting up to on the island.

Water skiing was thrilling. I eventually got the hang of it after a few false starts and falling in the lake. I took off like a swan gliding across the lake on my fifth attempt. Well, this was the impression I had of myself in my head. The others seemed to pick up the skill quickly too. We had good balancing skills. I heard laughter from Jack, Dan, Keith, Sandra, and Jess. Mike was already a pro. He had given us a demonstration. Waving to us as he skimmed the water. Everything he did made me weak at the knees.

The relief of having fun and letting our guard down was therapeutic.

I squealed at the thrill as we skidded across the water at speed. The wind whipped me on the face, and I felt alive. I managed three good runs, keeping afloat until eventually my strength gave way, and I fell into the water. It blew away the dreadful happenings of the last few days.

The skipper complimented me on my quick learning. However, I noted he was very complimentary to Jess. She looked like a different person from the one I had first met. She stood there chatting with the skipper, and lots of eye contact and laughter unfolded. When we had refreshments afterwards, they were still remarkably close. Mike noted it too and nodded to me; he understood exactly what I was thinking.

"We can do this often!" Miked smiled, "Since you will be a pro soon!"

I could spend eternity doing anything with you!

"I'll happily do things often with you, Mike!" I flashed a naughty smile back at him.

And he looked back at me, and I wanted to get naked right there and then.

Keith and Sandra were different after their water skiing experience. I had never seen them so animated or excited.

"It was fantastic," they both said together. "We were good at it, too!"

They sounded surprised that they were good at it, but they both kept fit by doing a lot of walking and hiking. I wasn't surprised they did well.

I feel I was starting to like them, which was bizarre as I had spent many years treating them with disdain. My judgment of Keith and me as a couple clouded my ability to see them together as a good thing. It wasn't jealousy that made me like this; it was due to the relationship between Keith and me that I wouldn't allow myself to see past it. Just because Keith and I didn't work as a couple didn't mean we couldn't work outside of that. I should've known this from when we first met and did get on. However, I allowed myself to forget our good times before living under the same roof wore us down.

On this break, I had learned much about myself—the person I was versus the person I thought I was. I now had to admit that Keith and Sandra were lovely people who were always good to my boys. They had cared enough to come here when they didn't even know how dire the situation might be. I needed to cut them slack from now on and be nice to them.

I stood up and gave them both a hug.

"I'm so glad you enjoyed yourself," I said. "You both deserve the fun after putting yourselves through this weekend. Thank you for being here. We've not always been on the best terms, which is mostly my fault. You're great to the boys."

My niceness took Keith and Sandra by surprise. However, they hugged me back.

"We always meant to come to Italy anyway!" they said together, adding, "But we wouldn't have stayed at such a posh hotel."

"Iona, we're both to blame for our actions toward each other, but we have great kids. I'll try harder as well," Keith said. "You've never been one for a quiet existence, so thanks for the adventure, but next time maybe just some Theme Park tickets might do!"

We all laughed, and Mike gave me a fantastic look. As we walked back to the hotel hand in hand, Mike said,

"That was lovely seeing you make peace with Keith and Sandra. Not everyone could say what you said or is willing to!"

I stopped and hugged Mike. "See what you're doing to me; I've gone soft in the head."

Then I kissed him on the lips in a slow, passionate embrace.

Chapter 29

It was Thursday. What a week in my life. Expect the unexpected, they say. Whoever 'they' is? Well, this unanticipated week was a tidal wave of emotion. To end the week by going to a glamorous Hollywood A-list party at Mike's villa was surreal.

Mike and I packed my things and headed to the villa on Thursday night. We left the others with instructions about when the driver would pick them up on Friday night.

Hairdressers, makeup artists, and personal dressers were coming to help Jess and Sandra prepare, while Jack, Dan, and Keith had to go to an Italian tailor to be suited and booted. They were all incredibly excited.

The skipper waited for us at the boat by the jetty. Mike had also invited him to the party and asked him to stay at the villa overnight. The skipper replied he was heading back to Bellagio to attend to chores he had to do. Then he winked. My heart sang; it seemed he was heading back to see Jess. If she found happiness amongst this madness, I would feel exonerated.

We sailed across the lake in the early evening sunshine. We didn't speak a word. Instead, we basked in the silence and peace we hadn't known in the previous days. It was meditative and much needed. Sitting still and looking out at the water calmed me. Mike and I held hands.

The boat approached the jetty at Mike's villa. Flashbacks to last Saturday night filled my head with dizzy notions about getting into the pool again. However, I knew there were flower arrangers, bar staff, housekeeping staff, and Emilio, turning the place into party central. I might need to behave myself.

We climbed onto the steps, and the skipper waved us farewell. We wished him a pleasant night. An excited Italian man stood at the top, shouting and waving his hands. Emilio didn't need an introduction.

"Do you see what I mean?" Mike said, "This is why I needed to go out for a coffee last Saturday to escape this. Thank goodness for Emilio, though, or I would never have met you!"

Then he splashed freezing water on my legs, and I shrieked. Emilio looked at me as if I were crazy.

Mike introduced me as his 'girlfriend,'
Oh yes fucking please, I'll be your girlfriend!

Emilio's attitude changed, and he smiled, kissing me on the cheek and expressing how much he loved my hair.

'What colour will you wear tomorrow night, Iona?' Emilio asked. Before I could answer, he said, "Red, it must be red, with your blonde hair and to be part of the colour scheme. Come with me right now to meet Leandro. He has just what you need.'

I looked at Mike, who was laughing. "You better do what he says, have fun, and I'll see you in the drawing room for a nightcap! Lorenzo will bring you to the right spot once Emilio and Leandro let you escape!"

Emilio led me back up the familiar stairway with the banister I had slid down on Sunday. The thought made me giggle. Emilio looked at me again as if I were crazy.

The event organisers had decorated the villa with gorgeous flowers, all in red and white.

Blooms adorned the archways and banister, and it was stunning. I understood why Emilio wanted me in red to match the décor. Who was I to complain? I was happy to be part of his colour scheme!

Leandro was a version of Emilio. He was excited and chatty.

"Come here, beautiful Iona," he squealed, "I'm so excited to dress you."

I didn't usually like anyone else telling me what to wear. However, Leandro opened the door to a dressing room with stunning gowns. I could agree to them bossing me around on this occasion.

Leandro pulled out a gown. "Try this one first!" he demanded. I felt he was definitely in charge.

There was no modesty here. They took my clothes off and zipped me into the red gown before I could think about it.

The gown was red silk, with a large bow across the bust and a diamond-shaped open section below. The waist then dropped with a ruched portion at the abdomen, flowing into the skirt with a sweep train at the back. There was a long split up the front left leg. The back plunged to the waist. There was no bra going on with this dress. However, as it was an expensive garment, the cut and the boned built-in bra under the bow held me in place beautifully.

I looked in the mirror and knew I wanted this one. There was no need to try on any others. I hoped they agreed because I knew I wasn't in charge here.

Emilio and Leandro then put gorgeous red Christian Louboutin heels on my feet. They stood back, looked at each other, high-fived, and screamed.

"Fantastico!" Leandro squealed. He clapped his hands. "Tomorrow, we'll complement the look with hair and makeup! Be here at 3 pm."

They had me unzipped and redressed before I could count to ten.

"Thank you," I said. They hugged and dismissed me out the door, where Lorenzo awaited me. I did blush as I knew he'd seen Mike and me on Sunday morning by the pool. However, he was a gentleman and a true professional.

"Lovely to see you, Iona," he said, smiling, then guided me down the staircase to where Mike lounged elegantly in his drawing room, looking as handsome as ever.

Mike handed me a McCallan and looked right into my eyes. I sipped it slowly, keeping myself in Mike's stare.

He had asked Lorenzo to close the doors on the way out.

The floor was marble. I sat down on it and pulled off my clothes. I lay out on the Marble floor, then I poured my whiskey over myself, and rubbed it in slowly. Mike never took his eyes off me. I could see how hard he was. Then he ripped his clothes off and came down on top of me, licking it all up. Kissing me everywhere he could, it was slow and erotic. We enjoyed every bit of each other, discovering all areas and discovering more about what we wanted and liked.

Mike and I set each other's worlds on fire on the marble floor. The tiles were cool against our skin, but the heat radiating from us made it the perfect storm. It felt beautiful and poetic. More than lust, this was so much more. We both knew it by looking into each other's eyes. Untold feelings rose into our pupils, telling each other what we thought. A bond had silently developed between us, even with all the bedlam that ensued.

We didn't speak.

We didn't have to.

Chapter 30

Friday arrived in a blast of sun rays from the start. The villa was alive with activity; food and drink deliveries arrived for the party.

Mike and I had a late breakfast by the pool. We had slept like logs in the giant four-poster bed in his room. I nearly lost myself in it. A few times during the night, Mike had pulled me back beside him on the giant mattress, as I floated around. I had many ideas about what to get up to on that bed when we had more time!

We went to the pool and swam lengths. It felt good to swim and stretch all my muscles. We managed to keep our hands off each other for once, which was respectable as many people were preparing for the party.

At 3 pm, we kissed each other goodbye until the evening.

"We will meet at the top of the staircase at 7 pm," Mike told me. Then you and I'll make an entrance to the party, together!"

I hadn't considered how I would enter the party.

"Okay," I giggled, "I like making an entrance!"

"More like a whole performance," Mike laughed, winking at me.

Then he spanked my backside, and I shrieked. He told me I better go before he started chasing me. I ran upstairs giggling. What a way to act in your forties, I loved it!

"7 pm," he shouted after me.

I blew him a kiss from the top of the stairs before entering Emilio and Leandro's world!

I went into the dressing room. Leandro hugged me, then said, "Let us get to work here!"

I laughed inwardly as if I needed lots of work; you wouldn't need to have taken offence easily!

They rubbed, scrubbed, washed, moisturised, pampered, and puffed—hairdressers, makeup artists, and manicurists. It was fantastic for someone else to do all the work.

After two hours, they brought me snacks. Then the makeup continued. By 6 pm, Leandro put the gown on me. Then Emilio came in and made me walk up and down with the shoes on. They all jumped about, squealing, and were happy. I must've looked okay. I didn't know how I looked; at this point, I hadn't even looked in the mirror.

They guided me to the full-length mirror. They had made me look like a princess. I took a sharp intake of breath when I saw myself. You think you're good at putting yourself together until the professionals do it. They had complemented the dress with sparkling diamond earrings. The sparkles dazzled me.

They took photographs, and I was thrilled to pose for them. I was excited to see Mike.

When 7 pm arrived, Lorenzo came to the door. Leandro ushered me out. Emilio had long gone to give the staff their final instructions.

Lorenzo offered me his arm.

"You look stunning, Iona."

"Thank you, Lorenzo," I replied, smiling.

Lorenzo led me along the hallway. Mike stood there. A handsome vision in a black tuxedo, white shirt, and bow tie. He was gorgeous. His smile lit up the whole place as I walked towards him.

"I can hardly speak, Iona. You're beyond stunning," he said. His voice shook.

He took my hand and kissed it. Then he regained his composure.

Putting out his arm, he said, "Shall we?"

I giggled and took his arm, "You're a handsome devil, Mike."

He smiled and winked at me.

We proceeded to the top of the stairs. It was a dream.

I looked down, and there was a sea of faces—famous faces, faces I recognised from movies and TV. Then my eyes saw my two gorgeous boys. They were kitted out in black suits, and I was ecstatic when I saw them. They were so handsome. They were both looking up at me, grinning with approval. I smiled back at them. I was so proud of my boys.

Then, it couldn't be. Keith and Sandra were beside them! Wow, they looked great, very regal, and pleased with themselves. Sandra looked stunning. It was great to see her in a less sensible persona.

Then I caught sight of Jess and the skipper. She was radiant and looked like a new woman. The skipper was beside her, and they were laughing and joking.

This was a spectacular scene.

I looked around. Mike was smiling at me. He had seen what I had seen.

All of a sudden, Emilio's voice came through a loudspeaker.

"Ladies and gentlemen, please give a massive cheer to your hosts this evening, Mike and Iona!"

Everyone cheered and clapped as Mike, and I went elegantly downstairs.

Thank goodness I could walk well in high heels.

There was cheering and clapping as we descended into the crowd.

We embraced my boys, Keith, and Sandra, then Jess and the skipper. Mike introduced me to many famous people. I smiled and chatted, Mike always by my side.

When we got a quiet moment, Mike whispered,

"You're an amazing woman, Iona, I love you!"

"I love you right back," I whispered. And I kissed him like I had never kissed anyone before.

Epilogue

Mike had stopped to speak to someone. I wandered over to the garden and stood by the edge, observing. I was thrilled.

I loved Mike, too; I knew we only met seven days ago, but I knew. I'd never felt this way before.

Everyone was enjoying Mike's party. People were chatting and dancing, generally having a fabulous time. I still couldn't quite believe it. I could see the boys dancing with a group of young actors. Keith and Sandra were chatting to a guy who does documentaries. And Jess and the skipper only had eyes for each other.

A waiter came toward me with a tray of champagne, smiling at me. I thought he was familiar, but couldn't place him.

Mike was still talking and looked good enough to eat. As the waiter approached, he looked over to me.

I took the flute of champagne from the waiter and thanked him, smiling. He smiled back at me, then disappeared into the crowd.

Mike walked over to me.

He said, "That waiter looked familiar. He looked like…"

"Antonio," we both said at the same time.

We both shook our heads, probably paranoid by all that had happened. We dismissed the idea, agreeing that a few guys in the area looked similar to Antonio.

We should've realised it was Antonio's brother…

To find out what happened next, Pandemonium in Prague is coming soon…

Acknowledgements

Thank you to my wonderful family and friends for encouraging me to complete this novel.

They've shared my updates and told as many people as possible to help me finish this novel and get it out to the world.

I'm self-published, so if you're reading this, thank you for buying or borrowing, which supports me and the other authors who love to write and put a lot of work into getting our books out to the public domain on our own.

Reading is for everyone!

Until next time, happy reading.
Arlene

For more information on my upcoming books, please see my publishing website at www.balloonificent.co.uk

Printed in Great Britain
by Amazon